Dear Reader,

Some of my most vivid memories stem from living in southern France. The breathtaking scenery. The dramatic archeological sites and art. The fabulous food and wine. The frustration of explaining in French over the telephone why I really needed to have the window of my ground-floor apartment on a busy street in Marseilles fixed immediately! Then there was the washing machine that managed approximately four items per load and took two hours.

I knew when I was writing this Flipside story that I had to incorporate some of my experiences. And while I didn't run across any mystery or stolen works of art on my adventures, I was lucky enough to enjoy the generous hospitality of the local residents. Talk about a special part of the world!

Hope you enjoy your trip to Provence,

Tracy Kelleher

P.S. I love to hear from my readers. Check out my Web site: www.tracykelleher.com, or e-mail directly at tracyk@tracykelleher.com.

Shelley squared her shoulders and stood up a little straighter.

"I know it probably sounds ridiculous to someone like you, a Count, but the real reason I decided, no, I *insisted* on coming here was to prove that I could venture out of my airless office, that I could abandon my boring life of picking up dry cleaning for my ex-boyfriend and having my best friend lecture me on which fork to use and not complaining when the coffee guy gives me the wrong change in the morning. Because I want to confront the world head-on, even if it means risking failure."

She was completely out of breath. Well, no one ever said confronting the world head-on was easy.

She waited for Edmond to say something. Finally, after what seemed an eternity, he took her clenched hand in his. "I don't think it sounds ridiculous."

"You don't?"

"No." He shook his head, and for the first time in the conversation, Edmond smiled. A real smile that crinkled the corners of his eyes. "I think it sounds…completely honest. And just like you, just like the Shelley that I find so…"

The French Connection

Tracy Kelleher

HARLEQUIN®

TORONTO • NEW YORK • LONDON
AMSTERDAM • PARIS • SYDNEY • HAMBURG
STOCKHOLM • ATHENS • TOKYO • MILAN • MADRID
PRAGUE • WARSAW • BUDAPEST • AUCKLAND

ISBN 0-373-44214-9

THE FRENCH CONNECTION

Copyright © 2005 by Louise Handelman.

This edition published by arrangement with Harlequin Books S.A.

® and TM are trademarks of the publisher. Trademarks indicated with
® are registered in the United States Patent and Trademark Office, the
Canadian Trade Marks Office and in other countries.

www.eHarlequin.com

Printed in U.S.A.

ABOUT THE AUTHOR

A former newspaper reporter and editor, Tracy Kelleher swears by the benefits of writing to a deadline, wearing Italian shoes and occasionally glancing at a treadmill. She lives in New Jersey with her husband, two sons and a dog named Jack.

Books by Tracy Kelleher

HARLEQUIN TEMPTATION
908—EVERYBODY'S HERO
949—IT'S ALL ABOUT EVE…
994—THE TRUTH ABOUT HARRY

To my agent, Paige Wheeler—the start
of a beautiful friendship.

And to Jean-Paul and Mimi—many thanks for
introducing me to a magical part of the world.

Prologue

W. C. FIELDS GOT IT WRONG, Shelley McCleery thought. All things considered, she'd rather be anywhere *but* in Philadelphia.

And that old adage about April showers bringing May flowers? Someone should have told the City of Brotherly Love. It was May and it was pouring buckets, enough to leave six inches of standing water at every major intersection in Center City. Shelley had actually *seen* someone attach pontoons to his wheelchair.

And, p-le-ease, if one more perky TV weatherman said the rain was good for the farmers, she was personally going to shove his Doppler radar where the sun didn't shine. "Come off it," she'd informed the cashier at Starbucks earlier that morning. "The nearest agricultural region is southern New Jersey, and nobody—I mean, nobody—cares about Jersey."

He'd nodded and given her the wrong change.

Now inside, things weren't much better. The conference room of Dream Villas Enterprises may have been dry, but it was so stuffy, even the philodendron perched atop the filing cabinet—a plant propagated to withstand the abuse of countless bank lobbies and orthodontists' offices—had packed it in more than three weeks ago.

Shelley could sympathize. It wasn't easy sitting in a room where the most distinctive feature was a beige filing cabinet. It set the tone for the whole office decor: cheap and nasty. Cheap, she didn't have a problem with. Given her pitiful salary and unpaid college loans, Shelley couldn't afford that kind of problem. But ugly—that was a whole other matter. Call her a throwback, but she was firmly of the opinion that the world would be a much better place if everything were rendered in tempera, covered in gesso and lit with a soft medieval glow.

Yeah, call her a throwback. She sighed.

"What was that, Shelley, dear?"

Shelley looked up. Sitting at the head of the conference table was Lionel Toynbee. Reading glasses slipped down his pencil-thin nose.

Lionel, founder and owner of Dream Villas, was checking the proofs for the latest newsletter of his travel firm that specialized in renting luxury European estates—estates that featured top-of-the-line plumbing against the backdrop of fading Flemish tapestries, grand marble staircases and massive gated entrances, preferably emblazoned with crests for families like Romanov and Medici, or even those parvenus, the Windsors.

"Shelley?" Lionel repeated, turning her two-syllable name into three, so that it became "She-el-ley." It was a habit that she found particularly annoying, second only to the measly salary Lionel paid her.

"The piece on the Montfort chateau comes across very well."

Bowled over by Lionel's rare outburst of praise, Shelley almost fell off her chair. But then she quickly realized the reference wasn't to her prose. It was about the seventeenth-century villa built on the ruins of a medieval convent on the outskirts of Aix-en-Provence in southern France.

"But take out that line about the cool, damp walls of the subterranean caves. They make the place seem old. I was just there recently, as I'm sure you recall, and the feeling was one of timeless grandeur, not moldy decay." Lionel tsked. "In theory, customers say they like atmospheric old things like caves, but they don't really want to know the details. Talk up the whirlpools in the bathrooms instead. More jet sprays, less caves." He turned to the next page.

"Fewer caves," Shelley corrected under her breath, the curse of having a mother who was a tenth-grade English teacher. She took her blue pen and deleted the line and was about to flip the page when her eyes rested on a quotation from *Madame la Comtesse* de Montfort herself. Shelley stared at the words: "To savor the snow-white blossoms of the almond trees that cover the hills in springtime is to tantalize the senses with a pleasure so exquisite, it marks the soul ever after."

She saw the passage was missing a closing quotation mark and was about to make a notation when she stopped and reflected. Would she, Shelley wondered, ever be able to forget the world of missing punctuation marks and experience a pleasure so exquisite it would mark her soul ever after?

The fax machine in the conference room hummed into action. She looked up. Was it a sign from above?

The cover sheet had a handwritten message scrawled in large letters: "*MONSIEUR* TOYNBEE. URGENT. PERSONAL."

"Looks like something for you, Lionel." She passed it across the table.

Lionel moved his lips as he read silently, then slowly lowered the fax to the table. "My God. Françoise, the *comtesse* de Montfort, has died." He removed the yellow Hermès silk ascot from around his neck and patted the moist sheen that had popped out on his baby-smooth forehead.

Speaking of baby-smooth, Shelley had recently discovered a bill from a society dermatologist in the accounts payable folder of her desk drawer. But the evidence for BOTOX injections and dermabrasion was beside the point, especially in light of Lionel's obvious distress—the ascot *was*, after all, silk. "I'm so sorry," she said. "I know you and *Madame la Comtesse* go back a long way."

Lionel strummed his fingers on the fax. After a moment he looked up. "Wha-at? Oh, it's not that. It's the chateau. It's aw-aw-ful! The family is threatening to take the property out of our catalogue before the start of high season."

1

"YOU'LL NEVER GUESS WHAT happened today." Shelley slid into the booth at the Down Home Diner and looked up. "Oh, Paul." She pulled a wad of paper napkins out of the dispenser on the table. "If you're not going to bother to wait to eat, could you at least not drip your cheesesteak all over the place?"

Paul Gufstavsen, the pride of St. Cloud, Minnesota, took the napkins and swallowed. "Listen, I've just come off a double shift at the hospital, so don't complain. The important thing is I came."

"From what I understand, you always were a bit premature." The comment came from the horsey-looking woman who'd just arrived. She gave Paul an overly sweet smile that was anything but nice before turning her attention to Shelley. "Move over, girl-friend, I'm starving."

Shelley scooted down while Abigail Braithwaite stashed her briefcase under the table and sidled the straight skirt of her St. John suit along the bench. Abigail had recently been made partner in a white-shoe law firm and was also an heir to a fortune based on little things—coal, steel and the building of the transcontinental railroad. So, naturally she could afford to wear St. John suits. Shelley's couture, on the other hand, was exclusively T.J. Maxx.

Shelley waved off the waitress's offer of menus and waggled her finger in Paul's direction. "I'll have what he's eating but with Cheez Whiz and onions."

Abigail nodded. "You can get me the same." She held off until the waitress left before flaring her nostrils at Paul. "Only a heathen—or someone from the hinterland—would have a cheesesteak *without* Cheez Whiz and onions."

Paul munched, undisturbed. "My midwestern heritage is a burden I proudly bear. Besides, I seriously doubt that cheesesteaks were a staple of your tony family, even if they do come from the area. Tell me again. Where exactly is the family estate located along the Main Line?" He turned a puzzled brow in her direction. "I seem to have forgotten."

Abigail sat up straighter, if such a thing were possible. "Stop trying to act the innocent. It's Haverford, as well you know, having visited more than once when you and Shelley were what I can only euphemistically call *an item*. Thank God she saw the error of her ways and told you to take your little stethoscope elsewhere."

Shelley cleared her throat to restore order. "Abby, stop picking on Paul. Anyway, as you well know, our breakup was entirely amicable." Translation: she no longer got sex, but she still picked up his dry cleaning.

Not that Shelley's comments would in any way establish a permanent détente. To say that Abby, her best friend, did not get along with Paul was the understatement of the year. Even Abigail's initial evaluation had been less than enthusiastic. "I can understand the appeal of his blond, Scandinavian good looks and his above-average intelligence, but beyond that—I mean, if he's going to be a doctor, does he have to be an ear, nose and throat specialist?"

And when Shelley related these comments back to Paul—she had been in that stage of their relationship when she thought they should share all—he had responded, "I don't know where she comes off criticizing me. Not when she talks about going to Brandeis instead of Bryn Mawr as her act of rebellion—a gesture undoubtedly lost on the vast majority of the population. Hell—" a rare example of Paul blaspheming and evidence of his rancor "—*I* don't even get it."

The relationship had only deteriorated over time. No matter. She needed their attention—divided or otherwise—now.

"If you two ever stopped to listen to yourselves, you'd realize you sound like something out of a bad Tennessee Williams play—without benefit of an intermission," Shelley forged on. "And I really need you to focus on something else for a change—me."

Abigail sniffed. Paul gazed at his food.

Shelley nodded. "Good. Thank you. It's like this. I wanted to talk to you because I just found out today that the *comtesse* died."

Paul looked up. "Which one was she? The condo on the Algarve or the villa in the Piedmont?"

"Paul, we're talking about a woman who recently died. She was more than just a piece of property."

He picked up his cheesesteak and took a healthy bite. "Shelley, I'm a doctor. I see death every day."

Shelley seriously wondered if Paul witnessed death every day in an ear-nose-and-throat residency, but she didn't press the point. It wasn't worth it—much as their relationship hadn't been, either.

Abigail patted her hand. "I'm sure it was very upsetting. A donation to a charity of the family's choice is always appropriate." She leaned back and smiled benevolently when the waitress brought their order—it was like the queen at the grand opening of a pensioners' home in Bournemouth. Then she turned to Shelley. "So, which property was it anyway?"

Shelley started to mentally count to ten but quit at six. "The *comtesse* owned the chateau in Aix-en-Provence, north of Marseilles."

Paul paused in thought. "A quaint abode. Eight bedrooms, five and a half baths, four with whirlpool baths. Vineyard. Swimming pool. Riding stables nearby."

"As you can imagine, Lionel is totally distraught." Shelley said.

"I bet. He makes a pretty penny off that property and he's probably scared stiff that the family is going to pull the plug on the contract."

"Was she also one of his, you know…?" Abigail nodded discreetly.

"Lovers?" Shelley supplied the word. "I'd say it's a reasonable guess."

Paul snorted. "Please, Lionel didn't get his inventory by using the Yellow Pages. We all know that he's slept with or attempted to sleep with half the aging aristocracy of continental Europe—his personal touch has been in places you don't want to know."

Abigail shivered and looked down at her untouched food.

Shelley pointed a finger at her chest. "Not that I'm defending the horny bastard, but you have to admit the one place he's never put his mitts on is me." Being a naturally modest person, she didn't mention that while maybe not in the same league as Jennifer Lopez or Nicole Kidman in the looks department, she wasn't exactly chopped liver either. Auburn shoulder-length hair combined with a firm, rounded derriere and well-toned legs gave her a definite Julia Roberts allure—Julia Roberts with an extra fifteen pounds.

Paul shook his head. "Shell, get real. It's not like you have any property on the Riviera worth renting."

What could she say? McCleerys weren't Riviera types; not only did they freckle in direct sunlight, they lacked that essential je ne sais quoi—inherited wealth. "Okay, I get your point. But I'd still like to get back to my dilemma. You see, Lionel is intent on keeping the rental for the coming high season."

"Simple." Paul shrugged. "He goes over and wines and dines the *comtesse*'s daughter and weaves his usual magic."

"That is just so irritating," Shelley protested. "Why do you necessarily assume that some woman would agree to just about anything if she was showered with a little attention?"

Paul smiled smugly. "Ahh. I get it. There is no daughter, is there?"

Shelley conceded with a shrug. "Only a grandson."

"How old?" Paul asked.

"From the limited information I've got, probably around thirty."

"And Lionel's not considering extending his sexual tastes to members of the male species?"

Shelley shook her head. "No, not even when it comes to the Montfort chateau."

Abigail shifted in her chair. "So, what's the plan?"

"Well, the plan is still for Dream Villas to pay a condolence call—in person, naturally," Shelley said. "But Lionel's not going. He feels it might not be a good idea for him to resurface at a family event. You see, he and the *comtesse* were an item *before* she became a widow."

"Ohh. So, if Dream Villas needs someone from the company to go…" Abigail raised one eyebrow. Shelley nodded.

Paul waved from his side of the table. "Hell-o? Am I missing something here?"

Shelley turned her head in his direction. "About that condolence call…"

"Yeah?"

"Well, I've just been promoted from newsletters."

There was silence.

"Well?" Shelley looked around expectantly. "Any opinions? I realize this would be an entirely new direction for me to take. So I really, really want your input. In my own mind, I'd like to think I should try my hand at it. Expand my horizons. Push the envelope, so to speak."

Paul looked horrified. "Why don't you let someone else push their own envelope? Let *them* wine and dine the grandson and heir."

Shelley pulled back. "Don't tell me you're jealous?"

He made a face. "Of course I'm not jealous. It's just that you've never dealt face-to-face with clients. You're used to being support staff, handling the paperwork and stuff like that." Paul furrowed his brow sincerely. "I mean this with all the best intentions, of course."

Shelley blinked. "God, Paul. You think I'm a total wuss, don't you? No wonder our relationship didn't work out. And here I thought it had something to do with the fact I never made your mother's recipe for salt cod."

"Forget the salt cod," Abigail interrupted.

Shelley nodded. "Gladly."

"And to get back to your question, despite what the Boy Wonder here says, I think you're perfectly capable of being a front man—front woman, really. The thing of it is, you just haven't given yourself many opportunities to shine in that venue. Not surprising when you consider that family of yours." Abigail accompanied the last comment with a dismissive wave of her hand.

"Please, it's not as if I were abused as a child. Many people have parents who get divorced," Shelley said, downplaying.

"But how many people have a father who runs off to join the circus?"

"It's a common enough fantasy."

"For little boys, not for a thirty-five-year-old insurance salesman from Schenectady. Then there's your mother."

"Mom's not so bad," Shelley protested.

"We're talking about a woman who communicates with daisies!"

"It's bromeliads, a completely different family. They're epiphytic tropical plants—pineapples, for example."

That silenced Abby. But only for a moment. "I'll take your word for it. Anyway, it just proves my point. Despite growing up amidst these familial peculiarities, you've definitely got the right instincts. Just look how you extricated yourself from an academic profession that would have left you buried in library stacks and instead made the switch to the business world."

Paul snorted, aquiline nose and all. "Where she spends her time in a stuffy office on the phone with foreign repairmen."

"Ah, but what she does with those repairmen," Abigail said forcefully. "Do you realize Shelley's the only woman I know who can get repairmen to do what she wants when she wants—*and* in several foreign languages? Darling, with that kind of talent, you could run most Fortune 500 companies."

Shelley shrugged. "So I know how to say *sump pump* in French, German, Italian, Spanish and, if I stretch it, Portuguese. That's not the issue. What's really at stake is whether it's wise for me to drop everything—and we are in the busiest time of year for finalizing arrangements—and rush off to try to retain the biggest contract that Dream Villas has under what are extremely delicate circumstances. Why, just last week when I met with my landlord, *I* was the one who offered to raise the rent by three percent when he told me Medicare no longer paid for his mother's home health care. I mean, how do you think I am going to fare with a grieving French count?"

Paul shook his head. "You should have had me talk to your landlord. You always were too softhearted."

"But thankfully not so softhearted that she made your mother's salt-cod recipe," Abigail argued in rebuttal. "Salt cod! It sounds like something the Pilgrims would have eaten!"

"Some of *your* relatives, no doubt," Paul shot back.

"Enough!" Shelley threw up her hands. "I've really had it. I want to discuss something important to me and not have to negotiate between people who go at each other like the *West Side Story*'s Sharks and Jets."

"Actually, I always secretly wanted to be Chita Rivera," Abigail let drop offhandedly.

Shelley narrowed her eyes. "I mean it. This is not about you. It's about me—rather I."

"All right." Abigail shrugged. "You want my opinion on you?" Shelley nodded. "I think that you'll do a fine job. That said, you should feel free to call me at any time during contract talks to recommend tactics or counteroffers—or even things like what fork to use at a formal dinner party. You know these aristocrats—they're big on elaborate table settings."

Paul took a deep breath. "You want my opinion? Don't go. If nothing else, I don't like the idea of you out there all on your own."

Shelley stared at the checkerboard tiles on the floor and thought. "All right, then." She placed a determined hand on the table—first making sure that she wasn't about to dip her fingers in mustard. "Abby, I appreciate your support. I really do. And I know you don't mean to be holier-than-thou—you just come by it naturally, having spent too many of your formative years doing things such as pouring tea. But if I'm going to do this, *I'm* going to be the one to take charge of the teapot." Shelley frowned. The image was a little weak. *Never mind.*

She turned to Paul. "And Paul, stop feeling you have to protect me from myself. I realize, as the son of a Lutheran minister you equate love with pastoral care. But you never loved me when we were going out and you don't love me now that we aren't. You just feel compelled to enlighten me. As surprising as this may seem, I managed to do quite fine for almost thirty years before we met and I have managed to function very smoothly since we broke up. In fact, as far as I can tell, you're the one who needs help. Without me, you wouldn't have a clean shirt to put on your back. Really. Do you even know where the dry cleaner is?"

She held up her hand when he started to say something. "Hear me out. I've had enough of being the responsible daughter and friend, seeking out a safe but unfulfilling job, falling in and out of almost-but-never-quite love. I've decided to turn over a new leaf. A new kick-ass side is about to emerge." She paused, then smiled slyly. "And if the circumstances call for it, maybe even a wild, party-girl side."

Abigail's eyes grew wider. "Am I hearing what I think I'm hearing?"

"I'm sorry, what does that have to do with going to France?" Paul scrunched his brows in confusion.

Shelley leaned back against the banquette and crossed her arms over her chest. "Paul, you're a bright, sensitive fellow. Okay, you're not particularly sensitive, but you are bright. You figure it out."

2

THE MAN WHO EMBODIED THE meaning of *insensitivity*—and the staying power of French cuffs—sat behind his desk early the next morning. No surprise.

"I prefer to maintain Europ-ee-an time," Lionel had informed Shelley three years ago, when she had first started working for him and naively thought the job held the promise of glamour. "I find it cuts down on the jet lag on my trips to the Cah-ontinent," he'd said.

Shelley always thought that for someone originally from Perth Amboy, New Jersey, Lionel certainly had transformed himself into a citizen of the world. In any case, fortified by a *grande* cafe latte and a new sense of resolve, Shelley watched Lionel tweak the knot in his ascot. The thought of losing one of their principal customers appeared to bring out his obsessive-compulsive tendencies.

"So-o, have you finalized your arrangements to France?" he asked. "It's imperative that the company send a representative imme-e-diately. Just remember, the Remingtons will be out in the co-old if we do not secure the Montfort chateau."

She positioned the tip of an index finger on the table in the same way she had seen Carly Fiorina, the CEO of Hewlett-Packard, do in a newspaper photograph and leaned slowly forward. The position really killed her knuckle, but she didn't want to mar the effect. "I appreciate your concern, Lionel, and despite the rush, I can safely say I have things under control. First off, I was here until two in the morning making sure the office paperwork is ahead of schedule, and that means the arrangements for the rest of the properties won't fall through the cracks.

"I've also contacted everyone—clients, homeowners, workmen—that for the next week or so I can only be reached by e-mail. I've left a similar message on the company phone line," she went on. "In addition, I've downloaded all the relevant phone and fax numbers as well as e-mail addresses to my personal laptop, which I will take with me. I've also made arrangements to lease a cell phone with international dialing capabilities, but I plan to give that number only to a few people—you being one of them, of course—for emergency purposes."

Lionel nodded. "Yes, I'm glad you limited the number of people with the phone number. The ca-ah-alling fees on those phones are monstrous."

What a cheapskate. Actually, Shelley had been anticipating his reaction and she had purposely highlighted her fiscal prudence regarding the phone so that she could go in for the real kill.

She stood up straighter, accentuating her 34Bs. She

had chosen a tight, powder-blue cashmere cardigan with tiny pearl buttons. Ladylike but va-va-voom.

The corner of Lionel's mouth jerked in a spasm. Her mild walk on the wild side seemed to have an immediate impact. Shelley waited for him to swallow.

"I also contacted the travel agent yesterday and I should have the arrangements finalized today." She paused. "Unfortunately, given the short notice, it seems that tourist class to Paris with a transfer to Marseilles/Marignane Airport is sold out. Business class looks to be the only viable option." True, there was a Moldavian charter flight, but it was flying out of Baltimore via Brussels and it lasted something like eleven hours. Totally unacceptable for a woman about to embark on a life-altering adventure.

Lionel blanched at the information before finally nodding. "If that's the case, then by all means do whatever is necessary."

But just when Shelley was ready to bask in her triumph, Lionel hit her with information that made her think eleven hours via Brussels might not be such a bad idea after all.

"I'm counting on you, Shelley. Dream Villas has never needed you as much as now. Because, you see—" he halted as if struggling to get the right words out "—it's more than the Remingtons we'll have to worry about if we don't close the deal. It's the government...." His voice trailed off.

Shelley blinked. "The government? What's the government got to do with it?"

Lionel suddenly looked every one of his many

mysterious years. "The Internal Revenue Service has threatened to close down Dream Villas unless I make substantial restitution for what they consider to be unpaid back taxes."

"I don't understand. I religiously submit the business's revenue and expense forms to Bernie, our accountant." A nice man, even if he did send the world's worst Christmas cards—these atrocious paintings of Nativity scenes by, yes, his own brush, one step up from paintings on black velvet.

"But apparently you incorrectly submitted the information about all the workmen we've hired over the years."

"Hold on there. I submitted those figures just as you instructed me to do—indicating that the workers were hired on a per-job basis and not as employees of the company." Shelley took a deep breath, trying to keep panic at bay. She tasted stale air and remnants of Lionel's Eau de Sauvage aftershave.

"Apparently the IRS no longer considers that a valid arrangement. Not only am I supposed to pay the taxes owed but there is a sizable penalty, as well." Lionel looked at the tips of his tassel loafers. "You realize, of course, that your name appears on the correspondence to the accountant as well as on the checks." He looked dolefully into her eyes. "I'm so sorry, my dear."

"Considering the humongous size of the checks I've cut over the years—checks Bernie specifically had me make out to 'Cash' so that he could divide them among the appropriate agencies—you'd think he'd be able to keep up on changes in the law." The tightness that gripped Shelley's throat had nothing to do with the stratospheric pollen count. "Are you trying to tell me that I could be liable, as well?"

"I purposely didn't say anything before because I didn't want to worry you." He reluctantly shook his head. "I was sure I could handle the situation myself."

As if. The man didn't even know how to use the fax machine, and she seriously doubted if sleeping with the IRS investigator—Lionel's usual business ploy—would prove effective. "And somehow the Remingtons' rental is tied in with all this mess?" she asked.

"It's absolutely essential. The government has agreed not to assume control of the business *if* I can make a significant payment by next Tuesday. As the situation stands now, however, the chateau is unavailable for rent starting July first, which means we will have to return the Remingtons' money. And without that, our cash on hand is just too low—meaning they could start to seize business and personal assets imme-e-diately." He sniffed loudly.

"What about the money we'll get from the Nosenbergers? They're renting the place for two weeks at the beginning of June, and their contract is still valid before the leasing agreement runs out."

Lionel shook his head. "It's better than nothing but not nearly enough. June is shoulder-season rates, and their stay is wa-ay too short."

Shelley swallowed pensively. "Next Tuesday, huh?" She rapped her fingers on the table. "Even with flying out tonight, that only gives me six days."

Less than a week to bail out the business, keep her job and pay off her student loans. *And* stop her belongings from becoming government property. Not that her valuables would bring much: a coral necklace she'd inherited from her grandmother, a small etching that she'd bought upon joining the ranks of the employed, a spotty collection of mostly used art-history books and her Raggedy Ann and Raggedy Andy dolls.

"So now you understand why you must not fail in your dealings with the Montforts, for your sake and for Dream Villas'," Lionel implored dramatically.

"Yeah, yeah, yeah." She was beyond giving him support. As far as she was concerned, he was the one who had gotten them into this mess. She was of half a mind to follow in her father's footsteps and run away to the circus.

Unfortunately, there was absolutely no way that she could imagine herself in tights and spangles. Oh, well, she had wanted to spread her wings and take new risks—all by herself.

Unfortunately, it seemed as if the risks were being thrust upon her instead.

Maybe wearing tight blue cashmere hadn't been such a good choice after all.

THE FATE OF DREAM VILLAS and her own personal solvency resting heavily on her shoulders, Shelley slammed the door to her tiny Renault rental car and stared at the massive entryway of the Montfort chateau. For the first time in her life, Shelley had come across a situation where neither chocolate nor red wine provided a measure of comfort. Just as long as she could hold off the panic, she figured she had a chance—maybe.

She let her eyes drift above the heavy wooden doors to a carved stone tympanum. The ravages of time and intermittent Provençal rains had nearly obliterated the bas-relief, and she had to squint to make out what was left of it. At first glance, it looked like a lumpy pancake on a circular platter, but Shelley soon realized it actually depicted a squat-shaped animal surrounded by a raised medallion. A porcupine in full profile, to be exact.

"Just great," Shelley muttered. "A family that prides itself on its prickliness." Still, she had a job to do—and fast—even if it meant facing aristocrats who fashioned themselves after a spiny woodland creature. "I suppose it could have been worse. They could have chosen a skunk."

She reached for the heavy iron ring that hung at eye level and knocked. And waited.

And waited some more.

Tapping the tip of her black slide shoes on the pebbly gravel, she looked around. Enormous terra-cotta urns overflowing with red geraniums, blue lobelia and something yellow and vaguely daisylike edged the circular drive. To the side, an allée of stately cypresses led to a fountain, which splashed amidst mounds of lady's mantle. A low stone wall defined the garden's perimeter, and beyond, almond trees covered with loose bunches of white flowers marched in neat rows across the rolling hills. It was *A Year in Provence* come to life, only without the workmen in desperate need of a shave and long-lasting deodorant.

Shelley glanced at her watch. It was several minutes past the appointment time that she'd arranged over the phone. She raised her hand to knock again when she heard the crunch of footsteps on the gravel. An elderly woman walking briskly from around the back of the house came into view.

"*Mademoiselle* McCleery, by chance, is that you?" The woman's English had a sibilant French accent with a distinct oddity. The *r* of McCleery trilled off her tongue, reminding Shelley of an extra—a most unlikely one—from *Braveheart*.

"Yes, I'm Shelley McCleery." Shelley walked over and held out her hand and then realized she was holding flowers. "You're very kind to receive me. These are for you and your family." She handed over a bouquet of red and purple anemones de Caen.

"How thoughtful, and how delightful to have something colorful in the house. Unfortunately, we have been deluged with white lilies. One would think it was still Good Friday." She paused. "But perhaps that is appropriate after all—*Madame la Comtesse* always did fancy herself God's gift to creation." Her voice contained an hauteur matched only by the artful upsweep of her silver-gray hair. Massive, yellowing opera-length pearls like something out of a portrait by Rembrandt rested atop her black silk shantung dress.

"I am Marie-Jeanne de Montfort. I am sorry I was not here to meet you immediately, but you see, it is only the clients who inhabit the chateau when they are here. We—that is, the family—live in the cottage behind the chateau. It saves on heating and staff costs."

"Yes, of course." Shelley nodded, trying her best to follow the accented and somewhat convoluted syntax. One thing was certain; she recognized the name Marie-Jeanne de Montfort. The former count, who'd predeceased his late wife by a good fifteen years, had two female cousins who also lived on the estate, and it was one of them who invariably attended to business.

Marie-Jeanne guided Shelley around the main house to the cottage, which was nestled between twin apricot trees. Its multipaned glass doors were open to the warmth of the midday sun and white curtains fluttered in the gentle breeze. It was picture-postcard perfect—and also, by the looks of it, easily large enough to accommodate a family of six. The Montforts may have come down in the world, but one family's descent was another's dream come true.

"Isabelle, *Mademoiselle* McCleery is here." The Cuban heels of Marie-Jeanne's black pumps tapped on the cool tile floors as they entered the kitchen, where another elderly woman was waiting. She was practically a double for Marie-Jeanne except that she was dressed in a black wool suit instead of a dress. Her sole piece of jewelry was a moonstone ring as large as the average quail egg, which years of etiquette and an excessively large knuckle kept poised on her tapered finger.

"This is my sister, Isabelle de Montfort, *Mademoiselle* McCleery," Marie-Jeanne made the introductions.

"Please call me Shelley, Lady de Montfort," Shelley insisted. "And let me say I was so sorry about your recent loss. My employer, Mr. Toynbee, especially wanted me to convey his sympathies regarding the *comtesse*."

"Why am I not surprised at *Monsieur* Toynbee's sympathies?" Isabelle pursed her lips.

Marie-Jeanne passed the flowers to her sister. "Isabelle and I continue to take solace in that fact that *la comtesse* was merely a relative by marriage." She reached for a Sèvres vase and removed a cache of wooden spoons and a folded sheet of paper with typed names. Shelley recognized the list of repairmen that she regularly updated for each property owner.

Isabelle smelled the flowers. "Are they not lovely?" She placed them in the vase, filled it with water and set the arrangement in a place of honor on the table. "Though to give the late *comtesse* credit, you must admit, *ma soeur*, that she did have rather shapely calves."

Marie-Jeanne wiped her hands on a dish towel that was embroidered with a row of bumblebees— there seemed no end to the prickliness of the Montforts. "It is true, Isabelle, and something clearly not lost on Bertrand." She looked at Shelley. "Our cousin, the late count, was—how do you say?—a leg man. He once raised livestock, you see."

Shelley nodded. "I see." She didn't at all. "Your English, both of your English, rather, is—" she searched for the appropriate word "—remarkable."

The two women beamed.

"*Mademoiselle* Bruce would have been so delighted to hear that." Marie-Jeanne patted her pearls.

"She was our governess when we were young," Isabelle corrected. "She had a great fondness for shortbread."

You could take the girl out of Scotland, Shelley realized, but you couldn't take the Scottish burr out of her students.

The kitchen timer sounded and Isabelle opened the door to a giant oven and removed a large tart. "The, the, eh—" Isabelle turned to Marie-Jeanne. "*Comment dit on 'des mûres' en anglais?*"

Her sister thought a moment. "Raspberries, perhaps? I am not sure." She rolled the *r* and pronounced the *p*.

Shelley looked more closely at the freshly baked pastry. "Blackberries," she corrected. The last time she had had blackberries was when her family took a week's camping trip to Vermont to savor the wonders of the Green Mountains and maple syrup. Unfortunately, her parents had not known that May was blackfly month. Her father had abandoned the rest of the family soon after, taking the insect repellent with him.

Isabelle placed the tart on a trivet and smiled. "Yes, blackberries, of course. I thought we would have tea later, if it is not too much trouble?"

"Not at all," Shelley said. Food tended to relax people, and seeing as it was just tea, she didn't think there would be an issue over the flatware. In any case, it was the perfect opportunity to start the negotiations. "And will the count be joining us?"

Marie-Jeanne smiled wistfully. "If only."

Isabelle sighed. "That would be lovely, no?"

That would be lovely, yes, Shelley thought, seeing as he was the sole heir to the estate. "Perhaps you could call and invite him to come?"

Marie-Jeanne shook her head. "I am sure that he is much too busy."

Isabelle nodded. "His work, it is very important."

"And secretive."

"It occupies him all hours of the day and night — forces him to travel constantly from his headquarters in Paris."

"You make it sound like some kind of undercover operation." Shelley was intrigued.

Marie-Jeanne coughed and covered her mouth.

Isabelle pursed her lips and looked to her sister.

"*La pâte dentifrice*," Marie-Jeanne supplied.

Shelley blinked. "*La pâte dentifrice?* Toothpaste?"

Isabelle nodded vigorously. "Yes, toothpaste. International sales."

Well, whoop-de-do. The count might be concerned with the highly competitive world of tartar control, but she had the IRS breathing down her neck. Cavities would just have to take a back seat. "Yes, I can understand the pressing nature of his business, but at the risk of being rude, I really do need to speak with him as soon as possible. As I am sure you are well aware, the count plans to terminate the contract with Dream Villas."

The two women looked at each other, then back at her, nodding nervously.

"Please understand, in no way do I mean to be disrespectful to the memory of the late *comtesse*, but I was very much hoping to use this opportunity to get the chance to dissuade the count of his decision." Her muddled syntax was beginning to resemble the sisters'. Shelley hoped that was not a bad omen.

Marie-Jeanne waved off her apology. "It is impossible to be crass when referring to that woman. Françoise was no better than that Mary Astor character in *The Maltese Falcon*. How she treated poor Humphrey Bogart!" Marie-Jeanne's distress was evident.

Shelley's was verging on mild hysteria.

"You must forgive Marie-Jeanne her outburst. She is a true fan of Raymond Chandler," Isabelle explained.

"Oh." Shelley nodded, wondering if it would be considered rude if she asked for a double scotch on the rocks.

"My literary weakness aside, please continue," Marie-Jeanne commanded. "We will dismiss further mention of that woman."

The fact that no love was lost was becoming clearer and clearer. "Yes, well, let me explain. You see, I have always been a practical kind of person."

"Something we have also greatly admired about you," Isabelle noted politely. "The way you organized the electricians to come and put in those mod-

ern connections—*circuit breakers,* I believe they are
called—was exceptional, truly *magnifique.*"

"Thank you, but that is really just part of my job."

"Never underestimate efficiency," Marie-Jeanne
declared.

"Well, thank you again." Maybe they could write
a letter of recommendation for a new job if she was
unsuccessful in convincing their nephew to come
around? *No, best not to be negative.*

Shelley forged on. "Speaking of efficiency, don't
you think it would benefit the family to keep renting
out the chateau? That way you could maintain a regular income and have the satisfaction of knowing
that the property would remain in the family *and*
that you could still live on the grounds?" She stopped
to gauge their reaction. "I'm sorry, I don't mean to be
too blunt, and of course someone could easily argue
that my motives are not completely pure—after all,
the suggestion to keep the contract with Dream Villas also benefits me." *If they only knew how much.*

"You have nothing to be sorry about," Isabelle assured her.

"In truth, we were reluctant to interfere in the decision regarding the estate and burden Edmond with
our little problems. But we *have* been wondering
where we will go if the chateau is to be sold," Marie-
Jeanne confided.

"Then for your sakes and mine, I must tell you that
I am here in Aix-en-Provence only until the end of the
week, Monday at the latest. Therefore, if I am to convince *Monsieur le Comte* to maintain a business con-

nection, I must do it soon. Today even." Shelley looked back and forth between the two sisters.

Marie-Jeanne fingered her pearls. Isabelle toyed with her ring. And Shelley wondered if the two old women, who seemed more attuned to a bygone era of black-and-white movies and governesses, were capable of strong-arming their high-flying business-man of a nephew, who appeared to be oblivious to his family's needs. Perhaps this is what too much fluoride did to one's thinking?

Marie-Jeanne squared her narrow shoulders and stood up even straighter than before, as much a tes-tament to her moral fiber as to her upbringing. "Isa-belle, perhaps you would be so kind as to take Shelley on a tour of the chateau while I place a call to Edmond?" Marie-Jeanne elongated the pronunci-ation of her name—Shell-ee—in a charming and very un-Lionel way. She started to leave but stopped. "If I may be so bold, may I inquire as to your relation-ship with *Monsieur* Toynbee?"

Shelley straightened her back—in horror and as a testament to *her* passing the President's Fitness Test in middle school three years running. "He's my em-ployer, nothing more, I can assure you." And possi-bly not my employer for much longer—though Shelley didn't add that part.

Isabelle beamed at her sister. "You see, I said she was remarkable." She turned to Shelley. "For you, it is the Botticelli and nothing less."

3

ACTUALLY IT WAS MORE.

First came the chateau's library, with hundreds of leather-bound volumes—a books-by-the-yard fantasy come true. Only these looked as if someone had used them for more than decoration.

Someone had.

"As a young boy, Edmond, the new count, spent many hours reading the works of Thucydides and Virgil—in the original Greek and Latin, of course," Isabelle explained with a sweep of the hand.

"Was *Mademoiselle* Bruce his tutor, as well?" Shelley asked somewhat distractedly. She had just noticed what appeared to be a Gutenberg bible.

"Oh, no; *Mademoiselle* Bruce had already returned to her native Glasgow. Edmond mastered Greek on his own when he was recuperating from a fall from the oak tree behind the stables. He was pretending to be Rinaldo from *Gerusalemme*, off to fight the Saracens. You know the poem by Tasso, of course?"

Shelley shook her head. "I know of it, that's all." How many people could claim intimate knowledge of the epic Renaissance poem?

"Not to worry. Edmond can introduce it to you."
Isabelle smiled in that knowing way that immediately made Shelley suspicious. "Here, this way is to the Botticelli." She pointed to the door on the opposite side of the room.

They glided along the marble floors into a large room with flaking, pale-green plaster walls. Fading Belgian tapestries depicting beheadings lined one wall, and atop a massive rococo sideboard sat a pair of matching Ming vases. Shelley bypassed those in favor of the art on the facing wall. There was a small panel painting of St. George, which to her trained eye appeared to be a Duccio. Next to it and practically hidden by heavy velvet curtains hung a delicately carved ivory. She turned to Isabelle. "Is it northern French? Fourteenth century perhaps?"

Isabelle squinted. "I had forgotten about that *objet*. It is so small, no?"

Small, yes, but definitely to die for. Roughly two inches by six inches, it depicted a pair of lions, male and female, cavorting in a forest under the watchful eye of exotic birds and small rodentlike creatures.

"But it's so delightful, and a shame that it's not better displayed." Shelley loved the ivory—immediately. More than loved it. She lusted after it with greater intensity than she'd ever lusted for anything, Paul included. Which, come to think of it, probably said something about their sex life. *True, he's hung like a Clydesdale, but he has the finesse of one, too, Shelley had once confided to Abigail after too many Cosmopolitans.*

"But surely you agree that the ivory cannot com-

pare with our Botticelli?" Isabelle stepped next to
what was clearly the family's pride and joy.

Shelley approached the large framed drawing. It
was a preliminary study for the painter's famous
Birth of Venus, in which the naked goddess of love
rises from a scallop shell, her blond locks cascading
over one shoulder. The thing of it was, the Italian Renaissance master had never been one of Shelley's
favorites—she always thought his women looked
like Valley Girls without the benefit of blow-dryers.
And now she was even more disappointed than
usual upon viewing his work up close.

"I've never seen an original drawing of his," she
said, searching for a remark that would not offend
her hostess. "And it's amazing that you've managed
to retain possession of these treasures after all these
years."

"Oh, they are not ours to possess really." Isabelle
looked genuinely shocked by Shelley's comment.
"We—the family, that is—think of ourselves more as
caretakers of these things. It is our obligation to preserve them for the generations to come."

Shelley nodded. She was beginning to understand
how the aunts could live a life of genteel poverty and
still be surrounded by priceless masterpieces.

The sound of a decisive tapping grew louder as
footsteps approached. Shelley gladly turned her attention away from the art and the pressure of good
manners.

"I managed to get Edmond on his mobile," Marie-
Jeanne announced. "He is rather busy right now, but

he said he would be free for supper. You will stay and join us, no?"

"Of course she will stay. In the meantime, we can show her more of the chateau, the other rooms, especially Edmond's room as a boy. And we can tell her more about Edmond." Isabelle beamed and clapped her hands. The oversize moonstone ring nearly spun around.

Shelley was jet-lagged but she wasn't brain-dead. She recognized a matchmaker caught in the thrill of the chase when she saw one. "I would be delighted to meet the count over supper. But until then I wouldn't dare impose on your hospitality. I think it would be better to come back later when I am refreshed." And when she didn't have to listen to hours of stories about a card-carrying member of Mensa who was totally devoted to oral hygiene. A saga of mind over molars.

"If that is what you prefer, we would be happy to oblige," Marie-Jeanne replied. "After all, we have much to discuss this evening, including the matter of the washing machine."

"The washing machine?" Just when Shelley thought she had a grip on the old ladies, they hit her with another zinger.

Isabelle held up her hand in a rare display of authority. "The washing machine can wait. The girl is obviously tired. She needs to rest to be able to enjoy the meal." A twinkle appeared in her eye. "I know—rather than have the tart for tea, I will serve the *mûres* to finish the supper. They are ripe and juicy, bursting with sensual pleasure." She formed a circle with her thumb and forefinger and kissed her fingertips with her lips. Her eyes narrowed. Her carefully plucked eyebrows rose provocatively.

And somehow Shelley didn't think Isabelle was reciting a lesson from *Mademoiselle* Bruce.

"Du café?"

Shelley opened her eyes and blinked through the intense sunlight at the waiter. *"Merci."*

He lowered the tiny cup of coffee to her table.

Two small sugar cubes nestled on the saucer. She unfolded the paper covers—as intricate as origami figures—and plopped the lumps in the minuscule amount of coffee. Then she used the itty-bitty spoon to stir. It was like a child's tea set, Shelley thought. And everyone around her was doing the exact same thing—in addition to smoking nonstop. Not to mention the women, who were uniformly wearing high-heeled sandals that miraculously did not hamper their ability to maneuver on cobblestones. Unhealthy but coordinated people, these French.

Shelley lifted her coffee cup. Against the protests of Marie-Jeanne and Isabelle, she had insisted on leaving, not to take a rest at her hotel but to drive to nearby Marseilles. More specifically, Chateau d'If.

Shelley couldn't help it. She had seen the schlocky film version of *The Count of Monte Cristo* with Richard Chamberlain at an impressionable time in her life— one of her older sisters had just described in gory detail what it was like to get your period. And memories of the TV and movie star—god bless his wooden performance—had seen her through many a sleepless night. How could she *not* visit Chateau d'If?

The sixteenth-century castle, one-time prison, was perched on a rocky island at the entrance to Marseilles's harbor, and it had inspired Alexandre Dumas's tale of vengeance and betrayal, wrapped up in a happy ending. Ah, the happy ending.

Shelley took another sip, finishing her coffee, and let the sugary remnants from the bottom of the cup slide down her throat. She closed her eyes. The stress of her current situation might be far from gone, but now, surrounded by blue skies and white cliffs—and under the influence of a sleep-deprived caffeine/sugar buzz—she could almost contemplate achieving her own happy ending. Even if it meant the IRS slapping on the cuffs and locking her up in one of the cells here on the island. Well, at least the view was better than at Attica Prison, not to mention the gift shop.

"Be positive," Shelley murmured to herself. "There is no reason why life can't imitate art." Though frankly, she could do without the vengeance and betrayal part.

She leaned back and could practically feel the freckles popping out on her nose. No matter. She eased off her shoes and let the little bones in her toes relax on the warm stones. And here in the land of little cups and little demitasse spoons and little toes, Shelley allowed herself to stop being practical and to stop doing things such as obsessively recalculating her checking account balance. No matter what she did, anyway, it always came out to three hundred fourteen dollars and sixty-two cents.

Instead she let the golden Mediterranean light wreak havoc with the elasticity of her epidermis. Like some silly sixties movie starring Sandra Dee as the American ingenue, she gave in to the romance of southern France and daydreamed foolish thoughts of happy endings and finding a hero with a big *H*. Only there was no way she was transforming herself into some perky Sandra Dee redux, thank you.

"Miss McCleery?"

She smiled wider. Conjuring up a deep male voice with a French accent was a particularly nice touch to her daydream. The sensual sound embossed her colorful images.

"Miss McCleery?"

The voice became more insistent.

Shelley wrinkled her nose. It wasn't good when a daydream ran away with itself. She concentrated on retaining the mood. The heat. The languor. The big, oversize hero.

Then she felt a light squeeze to her upper arm through her sleeve. Her eyes flashed open.

This was definitely not part of her dream.

Or maybe it was. A big, oversize hero appeared before her, his darkened figure outlined against the radiant blue sky.

She rubbed her eyes. A man. No question about it. Definitely a man. A man in what appeared to be a white, open-neck shirt, its sleeves pressed by the light sea breeze against his muscled forearms. He wore black trousers cut to perfection over his narrow hips and long, powerful legs. And as he arched his broad shoulders back upon returning to his ramrod-straight posture, she immediately thought of Marie-Jeanne.

Well, actually, she thought of Marie-Jeanne for no more than a nanosecond—posture was only posture, and he was a man, after all. *"Quel homme!" What a man!* as the teenager had exclaimed in her seventh-grade French textbook.

"Miss McCleery?" He turned his head at an angle, and Shelley caught the sparkle of even, white teeth.

She shaded her eyes from the sun and stared. If ever there was an excuse to ogle, this was it. *"Oui,* yes."

"You were interested in the count?"

She lifted her chin, and with a slight smile that spoke of feminine wiles that appeared to have blossomed in the warmth of the French air, she replied, "Yes, I'm interested in the count."

He lowered his chin. And slowly arched one eyebrow. "Then here I am."

Shelley almost laughed. "Edmond Dantès, the Count of Monte Cristo?"

The corner of his mouth tilted up. His teeth glistened again. "No, Edmond, the Count de Montfort."

4

To say her mouth hung open wide enough to accommodate a small family of yaks was being understated. If the itty-bitty round table that held her teeny-tiny coffee cup were not blocking a direct path to the ground, Shelley would have been scraping her back molars off the dusty white pebbles at that very moment.

She rose, stumbling slightly as she pushed back her folding chair. "Count de Montfort." Her voice sounded reedy, thin.

"Please, don't get up." He lightly touched her forearm with his hand—a hand far larger and stronger than Shelley would have imagined for the leisurely life of a European noble. "May I join you?"

She stopped teetering only to become aware that she was barefoot. She motioned for him to sit, and he let go, leaving a warm imprint through the thin material of her suit jacket. Forcing herself not to touch it, Shelley lowered herself in her chair. She blindly fished around for her shoes and nervously watched as he pulled out a chair for himself.

What wasn't to watch? His jet-black, slightly disheveled hair curled over the white collar of his shirt. His shirt collar was unbuttoned—no, the button was missing. Nothing else was, though. Dark stubble highlighted his angular jaw and sculpted his too-prominent cheekbones. And then there were his eyes.

"You have blue eyes." She couldn't help it. Now that he was no longer directly in the sun, the color of his cornflower-blue irises was clear. Shockingly clear. Sherwin-Williams couldn't have manufactured a more startling color.

He raised his eyebrows, providing dramatic arches over the twin azure pools. "Yes, it's rare, but it is a trait that runs in my family, particularly among the men—and not always the upstanding ones, I'm afraid." His English was flawless, his subtle accent as melt-in-your-mouth smooth as a whole bag of M&M's. And as for his self-deferential tone—gosh, it was beguiling in a way that could get a gal in a whole lot of trouble. He might just as well have had a sign hanging around his neck that read Danger. Proceed At Your Own Risk.

No doubt the vast majority of the female population—those with a heartbeat and a passing knowledge of birth control—would have proceeded without a care, let alone major medical insurance.

Shelley, on the other hand, silently repeated her paltry checking account balance over and over as a way to keep herself grounded.

Seemingly oblivious to Shelley's discomfort, the count turned his head in the direction of the waiter and instantly got his attention. "*Café.*" He looked back at Shelley and pointed to her empty cup. "Another?" He smiled.

And at that moment Shelley forgot her bank balance, her ATM access number *and* the name of her bank. She shook her head no, not trusting herself to speak lest she blurt out something equally embarrassing along the lines of, "I want to have your first-born child and strip you naked—preferably in reverse order."

So rather than risk mortifying herself even further, Shelley concentrated on putting her shoes back on. She located one, but the other seemed to have gone AWOL. She poked around discreetly.

The waiter scurried off and Edmond studied Shelley. "So, Dream Villas has decided to make the rather grand gesture of sending over a personal representative to pay condolences?" He peered around the edge of the table. "I believe that's my foot and not your shoe that you've located."

"Oh, I'm sorry." Shelley immediately drew back her foot. "If you'll just give me a second. My feet were swollen after the flight, so I took my shoes off to be more comfortable. But now one of the little suckers has decided to make a break for it—kind of appropriate here, don't you think? Seeing as we're sitting in front of a former jail. Jailbreak? Get it?" She stopped. "I'm rambling, I know." And decided the best course of action was to lift up the tablecloth and bend down to find the errant flat.

And maybe stay there. Until the next millennium at the very least.

After a long moment, the count leaned down. "I was starting to wonder if I should send for a rescue party."

Shelley looked up and saw his bemused grin peeking from under the edge of the cloth. She straightened up—and proceeded to hit the back of her head on the underside of the table. Overhead, the cups rattled.

She pulled back and came to an upright position, rubbing the back of her head but stopping as soon as she saw him reemerge from below. .

"Your shoe?"

"My shoe?" She saw her slide in his hand and remembered what she had been doing in the first place. "Oh, right, my shoe. Thank you." As she leaned to retrieve it, a lock of her perennially unruly hair loosened from the barrette, which was meant to hold the thick mass of curls in an efficient twist, and it tumbled forward.

And *that* was enough.

That singular, insouciant flounce of dark red hair had Edmond suddenly reevaluating his first opinion of Shelley McCleery as a bland if somewhat clumsy American. Not that he had a negative image of Americans in general, mind you. Far from it.

Some of Edmond's fondest memories dated back to his time as a seventeen-year-old exchange student in Grantham, New Jersey, where he had enjoyed those quintessentially New World contributions to civilization—lacrosse, *The Simpsons* and Philly cheesesteaks. Ah, what bliss! Not only that, CDs were cheap by European standards, and female classmates were seemingly all above average in terms of brainpower *and* the length of their well-proportioned legs.

It must have been all that lacrosse.

Even more miraculous, a French accent allowed an otherwise shy bookworm, one who constantly fretted that he had yet to experience a growth spurt, to get more than the proverbial foot in the door.

Ah, what bliss!

Until the end of June, that is. That was when he'd gotten word that his grandfather had died on the eighteenth green of St. Andrew's Royal and Ancient. Since he had yet to putt in—with the distinct possibility of making a birdie—Edmond knew *Grand-père* must have felt cheated.

Edmond had felt cheated, as well. Gone was the possibility of lifeguarding at the Jersey shore that summer. Back he came to study for the *baccalauréat*, prep for the entrance exam to one of the elite *grandes écoles* and ultimately a career in government. Such was the decree by *Grand-père*'s widow, the last of his many couturier-clad and nipped-and-tucked wives. "It was your grandfather's last wish," Françoise had declared melodramatically over her third glass of sherry and just before she'd patted his bum when he'd been leaving the study. "He wanted you to preserve the family's long tradition of service to the country."

Frankly, Edmond figured his grandfather's last wish would have been that he'd go two under par for a full round of golf. Edmond also didn't cotton to being goosed by his stepgrandmother, whose face was so tight she could barely blink.

But in his own way Edmond *did* feel an obligation to the family legacy, a legacy—mind you, that included as many scoundrels and ne'er-do-wells as diplomats and statesmen. Given this latitude, he figured he was perfectly justified in fulfilling his calling in his own particular way—no excuses necessary, thank you.

Yet as Edmond held on to Shelley McCleery's slim Italian shoe—very fine quality, he noticed—he was struck by how much he really didn't want to think about his calling. Not when the shoe belonged to a slender, finely shaped foot which in turn was attached to a well-turned ankle—that being as much of her leg as he could glimpse beneath the table and below the hem of her trousers. And having never given much thought to having a shoe, foot or, for that matter, ankle fetish, the arousing images going through his mind were…well, really quite arousing.

He shifted in his chair.

"I'll take my shoe then," she prompted, holding out her hand. "It's one of my favorites, not to mention that I got it for a great price at Nordstrom's in Woodbridge, New Jersey, which, if you're ever in the States, I highly recommend checking out—not that you need to worry about that kind of thing."

Edmond raised a skeptical eyebrow. "You'd be surprised."

"In any case, ever since I discovered that my ability to hop on one foot for a prolonged distance was not up to Olympic standards, roughly about the same time I realized I would never be a prima ballerina, rock star or winner of the Pillsbury Bake-Off contest—I was still holding out for secretary of state, mind you—I became quite fond of wearing shoes on both feet."

Edmond hesitated before speaking and looked once more beyond the severe pantsuit and the prim hairstyle to the winking green eyes—rather startling emerald-green, he realized—and saw there was something quite unique about Shelley McCleery beyond the fact that she had mentioned New Jersey, the sybaritic utopia of his adolescence.

"My shoe?" A note of impatience tinged her question.

He coughed. "Of course. Allow me." And on the hard pebbles of the café's courtyard and in the ominous shadow of one of southern France's most imposing prisons, he knelt down on one knee and extended Shelley's shoe toward her.

She looked furtively around, relieved to find that the proprietor, who was leaning against the sun-drenched stucco wall of his establishment, was totally intent on deciphering the daily racing form.

"I feel quite silly, you know," she said and reluctantly raised her naked foot.

"You think you feel silly? Imagine how I feel?"

"Then why do it?"

He gave her a lopsided smile, and she noticed the button on the cuff of his sleeve was about ready to fall off.

"Why do it?" he repeated her question as he thought. "Because this may be my one and only chance to play Prince Charming." He reached for her foot with his free hand and, as he held the back of her ankle, slid on her shoe.

His head was bent, and she couldn't see his face, only his wavy black hair falling this way and that. It really was too long and desperately needed to be cut, or barring that, combed. She could think of any number of women ready to take on the task. "Actually, in your case it's Count Charming," she joked.

But then stopped.

Because his fingers were caressing the sensitive skin at the back of her heel. Should she say something, extricate her foot in some way? Did she really want to?

A noisy seagull chose that moment to swoop over and land on the ground in front of the café. It walked in its stiff-legged gait and poked among the stray sugar wrappers and baguette crumbs that had blown to the ground. From its purposeful stride, it was clear the bird was familiar with this exercise. It stopped a few feet from the table and stared at Shelley with its black, button-shaped eyes.

And just like that the moment was broken. Edmond let go of Shelley's foot and settled himself back in his chair.

She tucked her legs under the table.

He coughed into his hand.

She became entranced by the sea.

"Another coffee?" he asked.

She brought her gaze back to him. "No. No, thank you. I think I need to moderate my mix of uppers and downers if I'm going to stay awake this evening." She rubbed her finger on the Teflon-coated table-cloth, with its flower-print pattern. "Not to change the subject too abruptly, but I wanted to tell you how sad I was to hear of the death of your grandmother, *Madame la Comtesse.*"

"That's very kind." A note of formality descended over the conversation. "In point of fact, she wasn't my actual grandmother since she was my grandfa-ther's third wife. My real grandmother, along with my parents, died while strolling along the Prome-nade des Anglais in Nice many years ago when I was quite young. A Milanese banker, distraught at his mistress leaving him for the center-forward of the Forza Napoli soccer team, lost control of his Lambor-ghini, which jumped the sidewalk and struck them."

"How—" *melodramatic* seemed too insensitive "—tragic." There were worse things after all than having a father run off to the circus.

"Yes, well, they had just finished having aperitifs at the Hôtel Negresco, so I think they were feeling no pain." The way he worked his jaw belied the flip-pancy of his remark.

"At least you had your grandfather." Who later also died on him, Shelley realized. The layers of trag-edy were beginning to rival *Les Misérables.*

Edmond signaled to the waiter and pointed one finger toward his empty cup. The man reluctantly put down his racing form and went inside to make another espresso. "Yes, I was very lucky. And then there were my aunts, of course."

"Yes, Marie-Jeanne and Isabelle are clearly totally enamored of you." Shelley saw him frown. "What? Have I said something inappropriate? I mean, I hope you don't think I was forward calling your aunts by their first names. Isabelle insisted, you see."

Edmond paused as the waiter delivered his new espresso, taking away the old cup but leaving the bill. "No, it's not that. It's that most people cannot tell my aunts apart. True, there are two years between them in age—Marie-Jeanne being the older at seventy-three, not that she would ever admit that—but they look practically like *jumelles*, twins."

Shelley nodded. "Yes, but Isabelle's eyes are slightly wider apart and Marie-Jeanne has a small mole near her right ear."

Edmond leaned back in his chair and scrutinized her carefully. "Remarkable."

"Actually not that remarkable. It's just a matter of training. I once studied to be an art historian, so it's just that I notice details better than most people."

He continued to stare at her as he lifted his cup and drank.

Shelley gulped and turned to the water. She wasn't used to people intensely gazing in her direction. Even Paul had never gazed on her with such interest—the televised coverage of the NCAA basketball championship maybe, but never her.

Naturally, she did the only thing a gal unused to rapt attention plus lacking a discreet application of

Clinique light-as-a-feather but full-covering foundation could do—she turned a deep pink hue akin to a floribunda rose.

"You're blushing," Edmond observed.

"It must be the sun." Shelley diverted her gaze toward the dock. "Is that the ferry I hear?"

He turned in the direction of the small quay at the bottom of the stone stairway, then glanced at his watch. "Even arriving reasonably on time." He finished his coffee in one gulp.

"Actually I think this is the boat that was due an hour and twenty minutes ago." She slipped the small piece of paper with the bill from under her cup and fumbled for her bag and her change purse.

He reached out. "Allow me."

She clutched her beaded purse decorated with the face of Betty Boop. It was at moments like these—alien, foreign moments with a sexy, foreign nobleman—that Shelley could use some Boop-Oop-A-Doop. *"Monsieur le Comte—"*

"Please call me Edmond. Whenever someone uses the title, I have this feeling that I am being asked to meet their very eligible daughter."

On his comment alone she had no qualms handing over the check. Besides, it came to under the equivalent of two dollars, so it wasn't as if she owed him any favors like a quickie in one of the corner cells. *Hmm, a quickie in one of the corner cells…*

Shelley cleared her throat and replied, "I'm sure you suffer through the indignities of matchmaking as nobly as possible." She mentally thanked Betty

Boop for her outburst of Dutch courage and slipped the change purse back in her Miu Miu bag—a hand-me-down from Abigail, who had moved on to a monogamous purchasing relationship with Bottega Veneta ever since her promotion to partner.

"Are you trying to make fun of me?" Edmond asked, his voice aghast.

Shelley shrugged. "Only because you invite it."

Edmond pursed his lips and shrugged his shoulders—something he did very well being French and jaded, not to mention having very broad yet flexible shoulders. "You're right. Anyway, I shouldn't complain about the cream of female aristocracy throwing themselves at me. Luckily my aunts tend to fend off the worst of them. They have this inflated view of my worth—" if only they knew, Edmond thought "—and deem most prospects beneath me."

"Funny, I got the impression it was the exact opposite." Shelley had visions of Isabelle plying eligible women from Aachen to Zermatt with all sorts of baked goods. "I'd say their matchmaking skills are pretty well honed."

Edmond blinked slowly. Yet another surprise from Ms. McCleery. "You're saying…that my aunts suggested that you…I?" He made a circle with his hand.

Shelley held up a hand in turn. "Not to worry, your virtue is safe with me." *Her* virtue after a few more of his self-deprecating grimaces was another matter completely.

He leaned forward. "Perhaps this is something we should discuss further—on the boat ride back to Marseilles." He emptied a pocket of some change—retrieving a canceled Paris *métro* ticket that had tumbled out at the same time—and left the euros on the table. Shelley noticed he was a generous tipper.

She also noticed that even within the range of a friendly harborside chat, she was rapidly moving out of her league. She might have envisioned a romantic interlude with some archetypal charming count, during which time she pictured them both skipping joyously and seemingly weightlessly through the misty dawn—she clothed in a diaphanous dress of Grecian folds, her hair flowing about her shoulders and never in her nose or mouth, he in a white pirate shirt open to reveal a manly chest with a discreet amount of chest hair...

But maybe not quite yet. Not when jet lag coupled with fear was the principal force consuming her body.

Instead she assumed a businesslike demeanor, one that fit the practical side of her nature all too well. "Actually I'd prefer to discuss the matter of the Dream Villas contract—at dinner back at the chateau this evening. Your aunts have arranged it, and I know that Isabelle is quite emphatic that I taste her fruit tart." The less said about the implied aphrodisiac qualities, the better.

Edmond raised one eyebrow thoughtfully and appeared to consider her statement for a moment. "All right. Dinner at the chateau it is. In which case, I'll drive you back to Aix after the ferry lands in Marseilles."

Shelley rose, making sure that she had her shoes before she did so. "That won't be necessary. I've got a car." She walked across the stones in the direction of the ferry landing.

He pushed back his chair, its feet scraping on the stones. "You drove? In Marseilles?" he asked, quickly following in her heels. And very nice heels they were.

Shelley stopped, only to find Edmond looming over her one step higher on the descending stairway. A more defensive posture she didn't need.

She continued the descent to the sea—*not* a metaphor for the current state of affairs, she assured herself without much conviction. "Forget the driving. I found the parking to be the real challenge. Fortunately, I found this underground garage by the Vieux Port—" She turned when she reached the mooring and saw him hesitate at the bottom step. "What?" she asked. "Did I do something wrong about parking there? Isn't it safe?"

He didn't say anything. Just worked his jaw and did that staring thing of his.

Shelley felt her face go red yet again. This was worse than her eighth-grade dance, and she didn't think anything could have been worse than being snubbed at a game of Spin the Bottle behind the cafeteria Dumpster with the smell of sloppy joes and cigarette butts adding to the depressing circumstance.

She shifted her gaze and watched the deckhand from the ferry tie the lines to the bollards and slide a ramp out on the dock. Silently she moved forward with the other passengers.

Edmond stopped her by placing a hand on her wrist. And once more Shelley felt the immediate warmth of his body, the solid touch of his strong fingers. She looked down as his large, tanned hand slipped away from her pale skin. And she caught a glimpse of a gold signet ring with what she was sure was the family crest. *Prickly people, these Montforts*, she thought.

Prickly and disturbing.

Especially the ones with blue eyes.

"The garage is fine, I assure you. And if your credit card doesn't work at the *guichet*, the ticket machine, you can use mine. It's just that many people, even French people, won't drive in Marseilles. It's not just an urban myth that red lights in Marseilles are merely a suggestion as opposed to a command." His voice carried a mixture of concern and admiration. First impressions could be deceiving—especially when they pertained to Shelley McCleery, Edmond was quickly realizing.

She wet her lips and stared at the small dimple on his chin. It added a certain Byronic touch to his otherwise classic lantern jaw. "Trust me, if you've driven on I-95 north of Philly during rush hour—where the construction has been going on since the Eisenhower administration—you can handle anything Marseilles has to throw at you." Surviving the effects of his chin was another matter.

But she would do it—for her own sake and Dream Villas'.

She squared her shoulders and walked up the gangplank, resolutely refusing the outstretched hand of the ferryman. She was no wimp. She stumbled slightly going down the steps.

Edmond bounded up the ramp and hopped down

to the deck, ignoring the steps. He made his way forward as gracefully as Gene Kelly on roller skates. Did the man do nothing without self-possessed aplomb? Maybe he'd picked up his seafaring skills as a boy while reading Homer—in the original Greek, of course.

Of course!

He eased himself onto the bench next to her, the wind tossing his hair even more haphazardly across his forehead. He ran a hand through the front to pull it out of the way, but gave up when it flopped forward again. Then he casually placed his arm over the back of their seat.

Shelley tensed herself not to pull away.

He brought his lips close to the side of her head and spoke, his low voice rumbling through the din of the ferry's motor, the thrum of the waves and the squawking of seagulls. "After collecting your car, we will rendezvous back at the villa, on the terrace."

She angled her face, her nose in line with his mouth, and glanced up into those cerulean-blue eyes of his. There were crinkles around the outside corners that added to their charm. "You had something in mind?" She had to shout as the captain turned up the throttle and the ferry chugged away from the dock.

"Pastis on the terrace before dinner. After which we will just have to see what other surprises are in store."

Shelley was seriously wondering if now was a bad time to call Abigail for advice about table settings—among other things.

5

THE VOICE ON THE OTHER END of the phone didn't bother with a preamble. "Edmond, *mon ami*, you were right."

"The curse of being brilliant," Edmond said with the barest irony. Why deny the obvious? He might disdain using his title, but he didn't bother to hide his intellect from others.

The sole exception being his stepgrandmother. He had become adept at playing dumb every time she'd coquettishly uttered some sexual innuendo or let a hand stay a little too long in greeting. But then that had been typical—whenever she could, she'd laid her self-serving hands on anything connected with the family.

It always came back to the family.

"What and which locations, Vincent?" he asked his assistant in rapid French. He could speak freely, having excused himself when the call had come through back at the chateau.

"They found substitutions for a small Dürer at a *Schloss* outside of Salzburg, a rare Byzantine icon from a villa on Capri and a John Constable landscape that hung in a manor in Cornwall."

Edmond heard the flutter of papers over the

phone while Vincent read this information. He fingered his jaw. "But still no word on the latest switch here?"

"No, nothing's surfaced."

"Well, keep on it, and if you come across any others, let me know. Immediately. And concentrate on the assistant, Shelley McCleery. She's made an appearance at the chateau, and I'm not sure if it's merely a coincidence. I'll try to find out what her plan is, but in the meantime, you search the usual records."

"Are you sure she's just an assistant? Perhaps she's her employer's *nana?*" To the colloquial French for *girlfriend* he added a cruder term.

Edmond rubbed his chin. He really did need to shave. *Tante* Marie-Jeanne hadn't said anything upon welcoming him, but she'd certainly given him an evil stare. "I'm sure of nothing," he said with a sigh and disconnected.

A smoky-gray cat circled his leg and meowed loudly.

"Boris, you swine, if you're looking for food, you've come to the wrong person."

The cat twitched its tail, seemingly oblivious to Edmond's slight. It meowed insistently several more times, then sauntered across the patio toward the break in the garden wall. It stopped, peering over its shoulder at Edmond before traveling up the path.

"Hunting for field mice?" Edmond asked without expecting a reply.

But he got one. An even louder meow. And that's

when it occurred to Edmond that a hunter is usually silent when tracking his prey.

And that's when he took off after the cat as it raced up the overgrown path, skirting branches and bounding up the smooth rocks that bore into the side of the hill. Every few minutes Boris deigned to look over his shoulder while scampering on light feet. Until finally it stopped to rub its back against a bulbous rosemary bush, the movement stimulating the oils in the needles and releasing a pungent fragrance. The cat narrowed its eyes into crescents and emitted a rapturous meow.

Edmond breathed loudly through his mouth and gave Boris a furious look. "You dragged me up here just to watch you get off on communing with herbs? You really are a wretched animal. I have a mind to pick you up and cast you—" Edmond searched the vicinity for the least inviting place "—in that cave there." He pointed sternly.

Boris condescended to stop rubbing in response to Edmond's gesture, and Edmond would have sworn that the cat smiled. Not only smiled, but smirked.

And then, just like that, the feline bounded into the dark entrance of the cave, and from deep within emitted a series of arcing sounds, which sounded for all the world like *"Penses-tu qu'on m'y reprenne!"* So *you think you can catch me!*

Nah. Edmond didn't believe in giving human characteristics to animals. He glanced around to make sure that no one was around. That no one would think he was crazy for following a cat into the abyss—which he would be if he did.

But you know, he was a Montfort with blue eyes. They were born crazy. And with that, he bent down low, and went in after Boris.

SHELLEY AND EDMOND DIDN'T meet on the terrace as planned.

Still, she'd gotten a surprise.

"I believe the problem is the, uh, *tambour*." Isabelle approached the washing machine. Shelley and the aunts were sequestered in the chateau's laundry room. Edmond had wandered off when he'd received what was supposedly an urgent phone call.

Urgent, my foot. Shelley figured it was a timely excuse to avoid the responsibilities of home ownership.

Marie-Jeanne fingered her pearls like rosary beads. "It doesn't turn." The burr was particularly strong. Broken appliances seemed to accentuate her childhood instruction.

"The *tambour?*" Shelley asked. She studied the diagram in the manual. As best she could tell, the washer had forty-seven different cycles and took what appeared to be the better part of two hours to clean a load of four dish towels, three pairs of socks and two handkerchiefs—men's handkerchiefs.

She cautiously opened the top lid and stared inside. Instead of an agitating action, there was a drum. "Aha, *le tambour,* the drum. I get it now, it revolves, or is supposed to revolve." She skipped the pages on bleaching sheets and turned to the troubleshooting section. Shelley read out loud carefully, translating the technical terms from French into English. "It seems to indicate a problem with the motor."

"And you can fix it?" Isabelle asked hopefully. "As you know, the chateau isn't rented at the moment, but it is the only washing machine on the grounds. We have been forced to do our washing by hand—not a problem when it comes to things such as silk stockings and corsets but highly inconvenient for doing the *nappes*."

"Yes, the tablecloths, I can imagine." Silk stockings and corsets, on the other hand, were beyond Shelley's ken.

"We have even been forced to go to this establishment called a Laundromat. Perhaps you know of them? They have communal baskets to transfer the laundry. Naturally I believe in democratic principles, but to share a laundry basket!" Marie-Jeanne shivered.

Shelley lowered the manual. "Yes, I can see where that would be a problem. Frankly I have issues with the change machines—they always eat my dollar bills. In any case, the contract between Dream Villas and the late *comtesse* runs through the end of June, which means the Nosenbergers will still be renting in a few weeks' time. It would be highly unprofessional to have a broken appliance during their stay."

Isabelle winced. "About things broken…"

Shelley peered from beneath her brows. "The washer's not the only thing broken?"

Marie-Jeanne nodded stiffly.

Shelley tapped the side of her fist to her lips. "Okay, let's start by dealing with one thing at a time.

We'll get to the other problems later." She studied the manual again. "According to this, it could be the circuit breaker." She looked around and spied the box on the opposite wall. "No, nothing tripped there. Why should it be an easy solution when it's so easy to make it complicated?"

She turned back to the aunts. "I'm happy to take a look, but I must warn you, in all likelihood you're going to have to get a repairman."

Marie-Jeanne let her pearls drop against her dress. "That will be expensive, no?"

"I'm not sure exactly how much, but if it's a problem with the motor, that's a major repair." She stopped. "Actually, wait." She peered back into the large envelope and pulled out a card. "I think we're in luck. There's an eighteen-month warranty on parts and labor, and according to your sales slip—" Shelley slipped the warranty card under her arm and rifled around for the receipt "—yes, just as I thought. You bought the machine fifteen months ago. It's still covered."

"This means?" Marie-Jeanne eyed her askance.

"This means, you—or rather, I—just make a phone call to an authorized dealer." Shelley looked up and saw the worry in their eyes. "And it should cost nothing."

Isabelle adjusted her ring and smiled at Marie-Jeanne. "Remarkable. Edmond will be very pleased," she said.

"*Oui*, Edmond." Marie-Jeanne murmured.

Shelley observed a moment of silent communication pass between the sisters that produced almost identical arched eyebrows. Shelley had the distinct impression that once more they'd moved beyond washing machines. P-le-ease. If this afternoon's encounter with the elusive count was any indication, she was much more adept at dealing with practical matters than engaging in flirtatious banter.

So instead of contemplating the possibilities of tripping the light fantastic, Shelley turned her attention to the matter of whiter whites and brighter brights. She slipped off her jacket and draped it, her bag and the owner's manual atop the dryer. "Like I said, I'm pretty sure calling a repairman will be inevitable, but given that you're pretty inconvenienced when it comes to doing laundry, why don't I have a quick look? You never know." She shimmied the washing machine away from the wall, the corners scraping the tile floor of the laundry room like Edmond's café chair on the stones at Chateau d'If. Then she squatted down on her haunches and peered closely.

The aunts craned their necks to follow the action.

Shelley checked the electrical cord. Nothing out of the ordinary there and it was firmly in the socket. The only thing left to do was take off the back of the machine and look inside. Four Phillips screws held the metal panel in place. She stood up, noting the stiffness in her knees, and moved her jacket to get to her bag. Her trusty Swiss Army knife should do the trick. After disconnecting the circuit breaker, she got down to business.

"You won't hurt yourself, will you?" Isabelle asked. She cautiously placed one hand on the corner of the machine.

"There's no electricity running to the washer, so there's nothing to worry about." She loosened all four screws and looked around for someplace to put them.

"Allow me." Marie-Jeanne offered an upturned palm.

Trying not to mar the Frenchwoman's manicure, Shelley passed the screws. Then she jimmied the panel loose and set it against the wall. She reached up for the manual and compared the schematic diagram to the guts of the machine, touching various components. "Maybe if I had a flashlight..."

"In the process of major surgery?"

Shelley looked up and wondered what she had done to so displease the gods that when a handsome count just happened to cross her path, she was squatting on the floor in the back of a washing machine. This was not a scenario that lent itself to moonlight and romance. She said the only thing appropriate under the circumstances.

"Would you pass me that large flashlight over there on the shelf?"

Isabelle coughed. Perhaps she'd been expecting something else along the lines of, "Would you like to come down and take at look at the driveshaft with me?"

"Of course. I'd be delighted." Edmond retrieved the flashlight and lowered himself into the tight space next to her.

Maybe she should have asked another question after all.

"Where do you want it?" he asked.

Shelley hesitated.

He flicked on the switch. A bright circle of light illuminated her chest. And clearly highlighted her raised nipples poking through the thin material of her tank top.

Hmm. That's right. She'd taken off her jacket. Shelley cleared her throat. "Would you mind? The motor?"

"Sorry, I don't know the first thing about machines."

"A likely excuse." She motioned with her hand where she wanted him to shine the light. Her elbow clipped his arm.

Edmond shifted the beam. "I'm quite impressed, you know. Have you always been this talented?"

"It's more an acquired trait. Some of us are born to greatness. Others have it thrust upon them. In my case, the pair of needle-nose pliers in my bedside-table drawer guided me toward the path of home repairs."

"It was the same way with me and Virgil. The second volume of the *Aeneid* used to serve as the doorstop to my bedroom."

"Well, next time I need a few lines of iambic pentameter I'll know who to call. Could you hold the light up a little?"

She leaned forward. He did, too.

And this time the length of her upper arm grazed his torso.

"That's odd," she said in a high-pitched squeak.

He turned, the tip of his nose brushing her temple. He inhaled the scent of baby powder. So familiar and so exotic at the same time. "What's odd?"

She could name the old "nearness of you" thing, but she stuck to the obvious. "It's the motor. You see how it's off-kilter?" She raised her arm—the one between them, since the other held the manual.

He leaned sideways to get a better look. His shoulder rubbed up against hers.

She could be bold and hold her ground, absorb his partial weight and full heat, or she could try and tuck herself into the corner between the angled washer and the wall…. The terra-cotta tiles suddenly felt very hard on her knees.

There was a loud clearing of a throat overhead.

Shelley looked up.

Edmond looked up.

And the imperious head of Marie-Jeanne looked down. "There is a problem, my dears?"

"Oh, let them work it out amongst themselves." Isabelle's beaming face appeared next to hers.

Shelley struggled to her feet. Edmond attempted to rise. Somehow there seemed to be more arms and legs than was anatomically possible.

Assuming an air of authority—or as much of an air as someone who'd been jammed into a corner wearing only a flimsy tank top and a brave smile above the waist can muster—Shelley turned to Marie-Jeanne and Isabelle. They had backed off a discreet distance and were doing much twisting of jewelry. "The motor appears to be dislodged to the side for some reason I can't quite figure out. You didn't have someone else in to look at it, did you?"

The aunts shook their heads in unison. "The only workers in the chateau were the village women to help clean before the funeral," Marie-Jeanne attested.

"And of course Marius, the caretaker," Isabelle supplied. "But I don't think he would have touched the machine."

Shelley knew from past experience that Marius never touched anything without major cajoling. A self-starter, he wasn't.

"Other than that, the last person to stay in the chateau was *Monsieur* Toynbee when he was visiting the *comtesse* shortly before her demise." Marie-Jeanne breathed in sharply, depressing the sides of her nostrils.

The likelihood of Lionel fiddling with a household appliance was even less than Marius. After all, he was too busy diddling elsewhere.

"Well, in that case, I'm sure it is still covered by the warranty. I will call the manufacturer's repair number if you like?" Shelley had a complete list of workers on her laptop.

"And it costs nothing?" Marie-Jeanne clarified.

"Nothing," Shelley repeated, combing her hair back from her face. Somewhere in the inspection process or in unraveling herself from the inspection process, she had lost her barrette, and her hair had sprung completely free.

Isabelle clasped her hands. "Isn't she a marvel?"

Edmond cocked one brow and surveyed Shelley,

doing a credible job of keeping his eyes above her neck. Well, most of the time anyway.

"A marvel." He held up his hand, revealing her barrette. "Yours, I believe?" He laid the barrette in Shelley's upturned palm, his nails barely skimming her sensitive skin. The cool gold of his ring slid for a second along one finger. Just a second.

Really.

Edmond rubbed his hands together. "Now I think I'm ready for that pastis. All that strenuous labor when, really, as I already admitted, I am—how do you say?—all fingers."

"Actually, it's thumbs," Shelley politely corrected.

"No, I think I mean all fingers." The smile never left his face.

THE AUNTS STEERED THE conversation over drinks toward small talk: the weather—very dry, increasing the specter of fires but nonetheless good for the grapes. The possibility of the music festival in Aix being canceled again this summer—the labor unions, always a rowdy bunch. And the fact that Edmond's apartment block in Paris was considering installing screens in the windows—horrid inventions when everyone knew that fresh air in the night caused lingering sickness.

Shelley took it all in, only occasionally contributing, wondering when it might be polite to raise the issue of the summer lease. In the meantime, she was content to listen and try to keep her nose from crashing on the damask tablecloth out of exhaustion, anxiety and the effects of an incredibly large and potent pastis and water. The cloudy aperitif might look like milk, but it packed a punch, weakening the bones instead of strengthening them.

Maybe that explained how she managed to swoop sideways in her chair—defying gravity and interlocking vertebrae—to pet the giant long-haired cat that circled her legs in a cloud of fur.

"Not near the guests, Boris." Marie-Jeanne put the emphasis on the second syllable. "You must excuse the cat. He is old and spoiled."

"And originally Edmond's." Isabelle offered Shelley another olive from the tiny faience bowl. "Edmond named the animal after Boris Spassky. Such a masterful chess player, even as a boy."

Shelley declined the olive, not quite sure what to do with the pit. "Yes, I understand the Russian grand master was a child prodigy."

Marie-Jeanne beamed at her nephew, who smiled, appearing to enjoy their chatter. "She was speaking of Edmond, the present count de Montfort," Marie-Jeanne corrected.

Edmond coughed into his hand. "Only a master, not a grand master, *ma tante*."

"You are too modest." Isabelle waved her hand awkwardly under the weight of the moonstone. The ring, Shelley had found out on inquiring earlier, had once belonged to Napoleon's sister, Pauline Borghese. "In addition to his skill at chess, he was a terrific horseman, as well," she explained to Shelley. "I remember when he used to ride a magnificent white

stallion that he brought back from the Camargue."
These marshy lands at the mouth of the Rhône River
were renowned for wild horses and wild bulls, not
to mention wild men.

Shelley turned her head slowly to the count. "And
do you still ride and play chess?"

Edmond shook his head. "Alas, with so many
commitments, hardly ever." He sounded very world-
weary, as if overburdened by the demands of the
peasants and obligations to the court and such. "But
when time permits and the occasion warrants, I walk
on water, as I am sure my aunts will be happy to relate to you."

There was silence and then the aunts twittered.

"Edmond, you do tease us so." Marie-Jeanne
brought her fingertips bashfully to her mouth, a pose
that she had probably not struck since she was a
young girl and infatuated with the groom from the
neighboring estate, since demolished and now the
site of a giant Carrefour supermarket.

Isabelle patted his hand.

Shelley was surprised to see that Edmond looked
genuinely touched. That he was a charming rascal,
she had already figured out. But that he could be
charmed by aged and overly doting relatives implied
a level of patience, devotion one might even say—
emotions she hadn't credited him having. Until now.

Maybe there was hope in saving the chateau after
all? Guilt was a formidable weapon, as well she
knew, and he couldn't be happy at the thought of dis-
possessing his relatives.

And maybe now she had an explanation—other than mindless infatuation and major jet lag—for her intense attraction for Edmond. No, come to think of it, mindless infatuation was probably enough, especially for her, given that her last major affair—okay, *major* was overstating the case, but affair nevertheless—was with a man whose idea of romance was buying her pink carnations from the Korean supermarket around the corner, and then only when they were half price.

"There is only one answer to your naughtiness," Isabelle said, rising.

The corners of Edmond's eyes crinkled in a very boyish way. "You know I would do anything for you and *Tante* Marie-Jeanne."

Shelley pricked up her ears. For someone reared under the stern Scots Presbyterian eye of *Mademoiselle* Bruce, Isabelle nonetheless displayed a certain wild streak. And with Edmond as a willing participant...

She turned, silently dreading—all right, maybe hoping just a little, because she was after all a woman who could use a little jolt of more than just java—that there might be some obscure Provençal custom involving dinner guests and counts, something along the line of being forced to kiss under a sprig of lavender or some other indigenous piece of vegetation, and inquired, "And what's that?"

"Consommé."

6

Shelley was feeling confident.

Not only had she managed the silverware without any hiccups through the first two courses of consommé and fish quenelles, she even mastered the proper technique for use of a finger bowl. *Top that, Abigail!*

And after enjoying another generous sip of the full-bodied Pommeral, which naturally followed a rather delightful Pouilly-Fuissé—naturally—Shelley felt the time was ripe.

Though maybe it was just that the grapes had been ripe.

Never mind. The aunts were starting to look at her expectantly, and once she got over the paranoia of wondering if she had spilled red wine down the front of her jacket, she realized they were waiting with anticipation for a discussion of the rental contract.

Well, she was just the gal to do it, especially when Edmond had just provided a ready opening.

"One of these days, the gold leaf on the trim really should be restored." He sighed the wistful sigh of a homeowner—though true, most homeowners didn't agonize about the state of their gold leaf—and gazed around the mirrored walls.

In honor of Shelley, the aunts had insisted on eating in the chateau's formal dining room—an homage to the Hall of Mirrors at Versailles, though luckily without the tourist traffic. The light from the Bavarian crystal chandeliers ricocheted off the cloudy-with-age surfaces, and large French doors stood open to the evening breeze. Hefty gold braids, which would have made fitting wigs for Wagner's Valkyries, held back the heavy green velvet curtains.

"Speaking of household expenditures…" Shelley peered around the sterling silver centerpiece shaped like a Spanish galleon. The prow prevented her from having a full view of Edmond.

He was seated with his back to the windows. The lush black of the sky framed his angular features, and the intermittent twinkle of fireflies popped on and off like little flashbulbs—nature's paparazzi capturing the local celebrity.

"Surely it has occurred to you," Shelley went on, "that the rental income from the chateau will cover restoring the woodwork in addition to the other household costs."

"Is that so?" Marie-Jeanne marveled and took a healthy bite of her lamb *en croûte*. For such a refined woman, she had the appetite of a longshoreman.

Edmond set his wineglass on the tablecloth and smiled knowingly. "Ah, yes, Dream Villas' contract." His expression didn't show the immediate delight in broaching the topic that Shelley might have hoped.

"Have some more potatoes *dauphinoise*, Shelley," Isabelle offered as if to make up for her disappointment. "Though perhaps there is too much garlic in them for your palate."

"No, they're just perfect," Shelley assured her. "Really, I should have potatoes like this every day."

"It *is* one of my specialties," Isabelle admitted.

"Edmond's grandfather, the late count, always said it far surpassed anything one could get in Burgundy, despite that region's proprietary claim to the dish." Marie-Jeanne weighed in on the discussion.

"Like most Frenchmen, he was obsessed with food and wine, particularly proud of our local Provençal specialties," Edmond explained.

"Then isn't it all the more imperative to preserve Chateau de Montfort's fine heritage?" Shelley jumped in before they got further sidetracked on something else culinary, like the finer points of bouillabaisse. "Surely, Count, someone of your obvious business talents can recognize that the rental income could help provide the necessary funds for the chateau's operating expenses."

Edmond thoughtfully twirled the stem of his wineglass between his fingers. Then he raised his head and, tilting it to the side to see through the main- and mizzenmasts of the centerpiece, directed his gaze to Shelley. "Unfortunately, someone of my business talents can easily recognize that the rental income covers only the minimum."

He paused and looked between his aunts, who commanded either end of the long table. Their graying and ever-proud heads were as erect as the Christofle candelabra that flanked the sides of the table. "And even if it helps with the operating costs, I am sorry to say that it doesn't begin to offset the estate taxes." The distress in his voice was obvious even to Shelley, pleasantly numbed by a surfeit of alcohol.

Muted gasps escaped from fore and aft of the galleon.

Shelley stared at the small cleft in Edmond's pronounced jaw as he spoke. In the candlelight, the dark beginnings of his beard made the sharp lines menacingly attractive.

No, mustn't go there, a stern voice commanded in her head. Think of Lionel. Forget Lionel. Think of the specter of the IRS and her own financial neck.

"But what about the chateau's wines?" she asked. "Surely the yearly income from its vineyard must be sizable? The Montfort name is well known among connoisseurs worldwide. Hugh Johnson gave the '98 Montfort merlot five stars, calling it 'sublimely balanced and majestically powerful.'" Not that Shelley could afford the premium label personally. But she *had* used that very quote in the brochure.

Edmond shifted in his chair. The legs creaked, indicating the need for regluing—something else calling out for repair. "The bulk of the vineyard was quietly sold to a German investment conglomerate eight years ago. The dearly departed *comtesse*—" Marie-Jeanne snickered "—negotiated the deal with greater zeal than skill, I'm afraid, and neglected to ask for a percentage of future profits along with the continued use of the family name."

Isabelle covered her mouth with her slender fingers, the moonstone ring drooping. "Eight years ago, you say, Edmond?"

He nodded. "I'm so sorry."

"That was the year Françoise was particularly enchanted by the couturier collections, Yves Saint Laurent's in particular. Such a parvenu!"

Shelley wasn't sure if Marie-Jeanne was referring to the clothes designer or the late countess. Either way, with the disastrous news about the vineyard, she could feel her livelihood trailing off into oblivion, as well. "Oh," she said and reached for her wine.

"Oh, indeed," Edmond echoed. "If I had known sooner, there might have been some recourse, but unfortunately I only learned about the sale when I came home last week for the funeral. That's when Françoise's lawyer informed me of the disastrous state of the chateau's finances. No doubt he was eager to procure his sizable retainer as quickly as possible before the burden of debt wiped out the available cash."

There was more bad news, news he had inadvertently stumbled across while still digesting the lawyer's words. That shock he decided not to share, not yet anyway. The aunts could only take so much at a time.

"No one is blaming you for not realizing the situation," Marie-Jeanne replied, offering an encouraging smile.

"Yes, how were you to know?" Isabelle seconded.

He shook his head. "Perhaps if I had taken more of an interest in the running of the estate instead of giving the *comtesse* free rein, things wouldn't have turned out this way." Their unqualified support made his failings that much more difficult.

Edmond cleared his throat and looked at Shelley. She claimed she was here to renegotiate the leasing contract. True, the property no doubt represented a prime holding for Dream Villas. But surely a business of that type experienced the occasional hiccup in its inventory? In which case, why was it so imperative that she come now *and* in person to secure his agreement? Most people would have bowed to social customs and waited until a proper period of mourning had come and gone. Was her urgency somehow tied up with what he'd just stumbled across in the cave? Speaking of which, he must remember to buy Boris an extra tin of sardines, the good ones from Sicily. And as soon as he could get away, he'd share the news with Vincent.

For the time being though, Edmond studied Shelley's face, with its slightly too-long nose and enormous green eyes glazed from the wine and the late hour, seemingly so sincere and so innocent.

So how best to deal with the offer that Shelley had put forth? For now, he reasoned, the best way was to treat it at face value and answer truthfully, no matter how difficult. And it was difficult.

"So, as to renting the property," he went on, "there is no point. Given the overwhelming burden of the estate taxes and the long overdue debts, putting the chateau on the market is a foregone conclusion. And as a result, I will go down in family history as the count who was forced to sell, the one who failed to maintain the stewardship of the Montfort treasures. I told you the blue-eyed members of our family were not to be trusted." He laughed but nobody joined in, a general sadness having enveloped the room despite the comfortingly sweet smell of jasmine wafting from the terrace.

He offered a quintessential Gallic shrug, the mark of centuries of philosophical resignation. "Since I am hardly ever in residence, it will be no great personal loss, but I worry about you." He motioned his head back and forth between his aunts, who were smiling bravely. "You have been absolutely marvelous over the years—to me, of course, but also for all the work you have done taking care of the house and all the renters."

The deep emotion in Edmond's voice cut through his habitual hauteur, and Shelley could almost imagine him as a parentless little boy desperately in search of security and finding it in the bony though welcoming arms of Isabelle and Marie-Jeanne.

"It was our duty," Marie-Jeanne said, tears blurring her words.

"It was our pleasure," Isabelle added, swallowing with difficulty.

"Just as it is my duty and pleasure to take care of you now, and I am afraid I am not doing a very good job of it. But that is all going to change. I have been making plans."

Shelley leaned forward.

"I've already begun looking into the alternatives. Perhaps an apartment in my building in Paris?" he suggested.

"The sixteenth *arrondissement* is a very nice neighborhood, don't you think, *ma soeur?*" Isabelle said with much courage.

"Particularly convenient for the bookstores—I have long ago run through the selection of Raymond Chandler at the bookstore in Aix," Marie-Jeanne responded, knowing full well that she had already read every title by the late author.

"Or perhaps you would prefer to stay closer to home? One of the refurbished apartments on the Cours Mirabeau in town?" Edmond asked, again lacking his characteristic confidence.

"They have elevators, I understand," Isabelle said with an encouraging nod.

"And intercoms," Marie-Jeanne said with astonishment.

Their brave praise for technology touched Shelley deeply. She needed to do something. Immediately the ever-responsible, can-do element of her personality asserted itself. "Before you rush into anything right away—"

Edmond placed his arm on the table. "*Mademoiselle* McCleery, if you spend long enough in France, especially southern France, you will learn that nothing gets done right away."

"In that case, surely there is time to think of an alternative—to selling, I mean."

Edmond rested his chin on the back of his hand. "You have one in mind? Involving Dream Villas in some form?" The porcupine in him was definitely showing.

Shelley wanted to push the enormous ship centerpiece to the side but figured it probably required the combined efforts of twelve stevedores and a small forklift truck. Instead she sought out a clear view over the forecastle. "Not at the moment, but after a good night's sleep, I feel confident that I'll figure something out—or at least the start of something. Frequently, a solution is hanging right in front of your nose, and you don't even see it." She gestured as if unhooking something from a wall.

And noticed that Edmond was studying her closely. She looked down. "What? Is something wrong? Do I have food dribbling down my shirt?"

And that's when her cell phone rang.

"So-o-o, She-el-ley. Any ne-ews?" Lionel's yodeling tones assaulted her ears.

She lowered the phone and looked around the table. "If you'll just excuse me, I have a long-distance call I have to take." She pushed back her chair and stepped through the open French doors to the far side of the terrace for some privacy.

"I'm right in the middle of dinner now—with the count and his aunts. I was planning to call you in the morning."

"Some things can't wait until mo-orning," Lionel chastised her.

Shelley wrapped her arm across her front and positioned her other elbow against it. She listened to him carry on for another few moments. "Listen, I'm doing my best, but the truth of the matter is, the count seems dead set against renewing the agreement."

"Well, that's not goo-ood enough. Next thing you know, he'll have appraisers and real-estate representatives in, running all over the pla-ace. And those people are like vultures, poking and prying, putting everything under a microscope."

"Frankly, I'd have thought that anyone with any appreciation of art and history would treat the chateau with the utmost respect."

"You think the IRS cares about respect? The poi-oint is that things could get very messy if I don't make that payment soon."

"I hardly think the IRS has taken to hiring goons to make their collections," Shelley joked.

Lionel didn't laugh.

In fact, there was silence—dead silence.

Was there something else he wasn't telling her? "Lionel? Are you there?" Shelly asked hesitantly.

"Of course I'm he-ere," Lionel replied in a curt voice. Shelley pictured his ascot knotted more tightly than usual. "Before I forget, have you checked to make su-ure that everything is running the way it should at the chateau? I spoke with the Nosenbergers earlier today and reassured them that the arrangements were in order and that you were per-ersonally monitoring the situation. Perha-aps you're not aware just how finicky they are?"

As if she could forget? Shelley shook her head. "Well, the washing machine seems to be on the fritz, and apparently there're a few other problems. But it's nothing that I can't take care of."

"Well, call the plumber imme-ediately. The washer is absolu-utely essential."

She didn't bother to correct him that an appliance repairman was the one for the job. As if Lionel would even listen! "Was there anything else?"

"No, but keep working on the count." There was a pause. "You mi-ight not realize it, but there are many means of persua-asion—especially between a ma-an and a wo-oman."

The only thing that saved Shelley from gagging into the phone was the fact that Lionel had hung up.

"NO PROBLEMS, I TRUST?" EDMOND asked when she rejoined them at the table. His raised wineglass hid his expression.

"No, just Lionel—*Monsieur* Toynbee—wanting to know how things were going. Naturally, I told him."

The aunts glanced nervously back and forth. Isabelle quickly handed her a piece of tart, then held up a small dish. "It's always better with some *crème chantilly*."

Shelley viewed the green Gallé glass bowl shaped like a lotus blossom. Its contents, a delicately smooth white froth, could never be mistaken for Cool Whip. "Thank you," she said and took the whipped cream.

"You were about to tell us about your phone conversation?" Edmond prompted her, accepting his dessert in turn. "It looks wonderful, as usual, *Tante* Isabelle."

Shelley shook her hand briskly to dislodge a dollop of the cream from the serving spoon. It was a highly satisfying action. "Well, if you really want to know—not that it's any secret—I told Lionel that there seemed to be some initial impediments but that I was sure we could come to a satisfying conclusion quickly."

"Time appears to be a rather large concern for you, if I'm not mistaken?"

"Edmond, you do not need to wait for us. You may start eating," Marie-Jeanne offered politely in an attempt to lower the tension across the table. Isabelle was cutting the last two slices of tart.

"I shall, *ma tante*." Edmond smiled at Marie-Jeanne. "But I was just waiting for the cream. And *Mademoiselle* McCleery." He looked squarely at Shelley.

What the hell! Shelley decided to help herself to another spoonful. She flicked her wrist forcefully, taking immense pleasure from making him wait.

She replaced the spoon in the bowl, then extended her arm across the table, over the female figurehead poking forward from the prow of the silver galleon. The small sculpture's naked breasts swelled like ripe plums. Perhaps now would be a good time to go on the offense in the negotiations? She smiled. "To answer your earlier question, you're not mistaken."

And that's when *his* cell phone rang.

"EDMOND, I HAVE INFORMATION on *Mademoiselle* McCleery." Vincent coughed. His voice was more raspy than usual. This case was causing him to double his daily quota of cigarettes.

Standing in the dark gallery, the velvet curtains partially drawn and the lights turned off, Edmond found himself searching for a pack of Gitanes himself, only to remember that he'd given up smoking more than six months ago. As a fallback, he wrapped his fingers around the slim lighter in the side pocket of his trousers. The familiar action helped him think.

And thinking was as much a part of his job as anything else.

As an undercover agent with the art theft unit of the French National Police, Edmond realized from Day One that he had found his true calling. He could combine all those years of studying with an innate need for a constant adrenaline rush. In his youth, that need had spurred him to kayak the roaring whitewater of the Gorges du Tarn and climb the sheer cliffs of Mont Ste. Victoire without ropes. His aunts had claimed his recklessness went part and parcel with the blue-eyed gene in the family. He didn't deny it.

Now that he'd matured, Edmond had refined that recklessness, taking what he termed calculated risks. True, some might have called them extreme. The jagged scar on his shoulder was a visible reminder of a run-in with a smuggler of ancient gold coins. But to Edmond it was proof of just how much he needed to keep his wits about him. Now more than ever.

"*Oui*, tell me what you've found." Edmond spoke into the phone, anxious for further information.

"It seems *Mademoiselle* McCleery was once a graduate student in art history."

"She mentioned she had studied art. But what was her specialty?"

"European, with a concentration in medieval and Renaissance periods."

Edmond looked at the art on the walls—one wall in particular—and swore.

"She dropped out before finishing her degree from the University of Pennsylvania, which is in... Just a minute, I need to look at my notes." Vincent stopped speaking.

Edmond removed his hand from his pocket. "No need. It's in Philadelphia, the same location as Dream Villas' office. Any reason why she quit?"

"I haven't been able to track that down yet. But you mean any suspicious reason, correct?"

"I mean any reason."

There was a pause on the other end of the line. "I think you need to stay close to your *Mademoiselle* Mc-Cleery," Vincent advised.

"You just do your part of the job. And she is not *my Mademoiselle* McCleery. Before you hang up, there's one thing more." He'd been waiting for this moment. "I'd like you to know you're not the only one capable of successful legwork."

And in this case, he meant it literally.

EDMOND RETURNED TO THE dining room, and the smile that had crossed his face earlier had vanished.

"You have been called away?" Isabelle asked with concern. "Something urgent, no?"

Edmond nodded. "Something urgent, yes, but I am able to stay. In fact, tonight I am all yours—" he smiled benevolently at both his aunts "—and *Mademoiselle* McCleery's." His smile in her direction was no less potent but not exactly benevolent.

"You have a toothpaste sales emergency at—" Shelley looked at her watch "—at eleven-thirty at night?"

Edmond opened his eyes wide.

"We told Shelley about your job in toothpaste," Marie-Jeanne said brightly. "International sales."

"Very international," Isabelle joined in.

Edmond nodded slowly. "Yes, of course. I didn't realize you'd mentioned it." He looked down, taking particular care while he spread his napkin out on his lap.

My God! He knew his aunts had only been trying to protect him. He had once told them that in his line of work, the fewer people who knew what he did, the better. *But couldn't they have come up with something other than toothpaste?*

After he had ruthlessly flattened out any and all folds, he brought his head back up. "This time it wasn't toothpaste, per se." He was dangerously out of his element.

They all waited expectantly.

"It was whitening strips," he announced authoritatively, hoping his arrogant tone would allow him to bluff his way out of the situation.

Shelley started coughing.

Isabelle poured more water in her goblet. "The cream? Perhaps it was too stiff?"

Shelley took a sip. "No," she answered, lowering her glass. She sniffed. "I'm sorry. It's just…just that the whole idea of a whitening-strip emergency at this time of night strikes me as kind of crazy." She glanced around, waiting for someone else to notice the seeming absurdity of the situation.

Nobody did.

"*Mademoiselle* Bruce always admonished us not to discuss oral hygiene at the dinner table," Marie-Jeanne curtly informed her. Then she turned to Edmond. "Do you not agree?"

"I think *Mademoiselle* Bruce was a very wise woman, as are you," he acknowledged with a tacit thank-you.

And Shelley started to think that this was one of those moments when it was probably wise to call it a night and start afresh in the morning. She rose without as much aplomb as she might have liked but at least with both shoes on her feet. "Please, I don't want to interrupt either the discussion or the meal—both of which have been absolutely superb—but I'm afraid it is quite past my bedtime and I had best return to my hotel."

Marie-Jeanne raised her chin imperiously. "Edmond, your manners. Tell Shell-ee that she can not possibly stay at some sterile hotel." She rolled the *r* in *sterile*. "That she would be much better off to stay here at the chateau."

A lesser man would have been a quivering mass of etiquette insecurities. Not Edmond. Not someone who had been presented at the Court of St. James as a lad of seven. "Of course you must stay here. There are many rooms. You can have your choice." If she were to move in, it would only make his work easier.

"But my room at the hotel is quite lovely and right in the center of town," Shelley protested.

Marie-Jeanne shook her hand imperiously. "The center of town—that's much too noisy. Here you can enjoy the peace and serenity of the countryside."

"Breathe the delicate perfume of the almond blossoms," Isabelle chimed in.

Shelley winced. Isabelle would have to bring up the almond blossoms.

"It's settled then," Edmond announced as if by royal decree.

Well, maybe it *would* be more convenient to stay here, give her more opportunities to bend the count's ear and convince him to sign the agreement. "All right." Shelley started to push back her chair. "I'll just drive to the hotel then and retrieve my things."

With remarkable speed—or maybe Shelley was just remarkably slow—Edmond circled the table and held the back of her chair. "Please, allow me to drive you to your hotel."

"But I have my car, as I'm sure you remember."

"Nonsense. Edmond knows the way much better," Marie-Jeanne insisted.

"And it is so dark," Isabelle added. From her lips, it sounded more like the seductive call of a siren than a warning about driver safety.

"Shelley?"

"Yes?" She looked over her shoulder at Edmond, who was holding the carved finials of the high-back chair. And then it hit her. This was the first time Edmond had said her given name. From his lips, it sounded exotic. Alluring. A sophisticated caress. "Yes?" she repeated, staring up into his eyes, a crystalline blue that rivaled the color of the waves that lapped against the chalky cliffs of Chateau d'If. In their centers, the pupils were as dark and mysterious as the inky-velvet night outside. The combination was entrancing and foreign, evoking an almost alien world.

He returned her gaze, peering into her leaf-green eyes that seemed as fresh as the buds on the grapevines just when they started to open and offer a promise of the harvest to come. It was a color that took him back to a time of youthful expectations of laughter and love and the unlimited possibilities that accompanied both.

There was a pause, a silence.

And then he spoke.

"Your purse?"

"My purse?" She had a purse?

"I think you'll need your purse to check out."

That didn't sound quite so exotic or alluring. Shelley sniffed. *Silly girl.* "That's right. I'll just get it. But you have to promise me," she said, standing up straight after retrieving her bag from the floor, "tomorrow there'll be no other emergencies. It's only fair that I get your undivided attention."

One corner of his mouth turned up. "Don't worry. Neither whitening strips nor wild horses could drag me away."

Somehow Shelley figured they were the least of her worries.

7

SHELLEY'S EYES WERE CLOSED, but she had no problem picturing the image before her. She lay in bed. Her hands were spread through the back of Edmond's hair and she was easing him down. A long, slow breath, and she inhaled that hint of sandalwood that was so indefinably his.

She felt the crinkle of freshly ironed sheets. Was that Edmond shifting sideways as he rested his cheek on the pillow by hers? She wanted to run a fingernail around the sharp lines of his cheekbones and firm jaw, linger at the small cleft on his chin in anticipation that he would grab her hand and lavish slow, delicate kisses on the tip of each finger....

Shelley opened her mouth, hoping she wouldn't do anything embarrassing such as drool on the pillow, and—

RING.

RING?

Shelley grumbled in her sleep and shifted on her down pillow. Scrunching her eyes tightly together, she worked at recapturing the moment. The moment when she and Edmond would join together in rapture, their writhing bodies humming in tune to the drone of cicadas outside the window, the insects' insistent vibration a signal of their own sexual pleasuring.

RING.

Shelley's eyes popped open. Cicadas did not ring. She groaned and shifted her head to look at the clock next to the bed. Five fifty-six. In the morning. It was a time fit only for energetic farmers and practicing monks, neither of which were close personal acquaintances.

The phone rang again, seemingly louder this time, and Shelley blindly reached out and fumbled for her cell, which she'd left on the end table. Sinking back into her pillow, she brought it close to her ear, and with her eyes still closed, mumbled, "*Bonjour*, and this had better be good if you know what's healthy for you."

"So, tell me," came a cheery voice over the phone, "what's going on in the land of sunflowers? Has the influence of rampant commercialism stolen whatever naiveté remained in that glorious patch of France we call Provence?"

Shelley breathed in deeply through her nose, the fresh scent of sheets laundered with lavender water permeating her nostrils. "Abigail, you may call it Provence, but I call it the freaking crack of dawn."

"Yes, well, I wasn't sure if you were going to take an early morning run, and I wanted to catch you before you headed out for the day."

"P-le-ase, have you ever known me to take an early morning run?" Shelley rubbed the side of her nose.

There was a pause. "No, you're right. That's me. I'm

the one who takes the early morning runs, and you know, when you come back to Philadelphia, you really should join me. There's nothing as exhilarating as greeting the dawn while you inhale the chilly morning air."

Shelley flopped her arm back on top of her duvet. Actually, Edmond's duvet.

Isabelle had insisted that she stay in his childhood room. "It will give you insight for convincing him to renew the contract. Allow you to enter his psyche," she had said conspiratorially. Edmond had been removing Shelley's bags from the car at the time and hadn't heard the coaching.

"And you know how we are counting on you to persuade him," Marie-Jeanne had added with more than a hint of desperation.

Great. That was all Shelley had needed. More pressure. She'd looked around the room, taking in the model airplanes hanging from the high ceilings over the dark four-poster bed. Old school texts and notebooks and a collection of fossils filled the shelves. A marble bust of some Roman senator stood atop a waist-high pedestal in one corner, and a thick, leather-bound tome held open the door. Shelley had peered closely at the spine, read the title and blanched. It was the *Kamasutra*, not the *Aeneid*, as she'd remembered him saying earlier. His tastes appeared to have matured with age.

Shelley had looked up. "But where is Edmond going to sleep?" She'd been a little concerned.

"Why, in the count's room," Marie-Jeanne had replied matter-of-factly.

"Oh, right." *Dumb question*. He was no longer a boy but the man of the house.

"So, have you been successful?" Abigail's question brought Shelley back to the present—the very early present.

"What? With the multiple sets of silverware?" Shelley understood Abigail's priorities. "Emily Post would have been proud. I conquered them like a pro."

"Well, yes, that, but also—"

"Oh, you mean finger bowls. That, too, I passed with flying colors, and I hadn't even gotten to that chapter of the book."

"That's magnificent, and to tell you frankly, only my second cousin Harriet, one generation removed, still insists on finger bowls, and that's only when she serves lobster. You didn't have lobster, did you?"

Shelley rubbed her eyes. "Did you call to get a complete rundown of my menus since my feet touched French soil?"

"No, sorry. I got sidetracked. That seems to be happening to me a lot lately. Like the way I ran into Paul earlier tonight."

Shelley opened her eyes wide and sat up straight. The duvet fell away to reveal her U Penn T-shirt, much washed and much loved. "You ran into Paul? Where?" Just because she didn't have a "thing" for her ex-boyfriend didn't mean she wasn't intently curious about his after-hours activities.

"There was this fund-raiser for the children's hospital—black tie optional."

Shelley flopped back on the pillow. "So, Paul was at a hospital charity thing. Big deal—he's a doctor. He's expected to show up."

"But on the arm of a female anesthesiologist whose breasts didn't so much billow as make a beachhead landing over the plate of crudités? Talk about artificially enhanced. Wouldn't a doctor think of the potential medical risks when considering getting breast implants?"

"Abigail, I don't think medical risks were the prime consideration in making her decision—something that I am sure was not lost on Paul and every other male in a two-block radius. Besides, he's free to come with whomever he wants." Shelley couldn't help gazing down at her own chest, wondering if her nipples were starting to point just a bit south. She pulled back her shoulders, making sure they pointed far above the equator.

"But that's just it. He *didn't* come with her. Apparently she'd latched on to him, and he was completely desperate to disengage himself—so desperate that he even resorted to chatting with me the whole evening. Can you believe it?"

"To tell you the truth, no. Coming to blows is more like it." She shifted on the mattress, snuggling into a more comfortable position. "So, other than a rundown of the latest society event and making sure that I haven't committed any egregious social gaffes thus far, was there anything else you wanted to talk about, or am I permitted to go back to sleep and pretend this conversation never happened?"

Not to mention, get on with my dreaming, Shelley thought.

"Mock me all you want. This call was meant to be about you. Besides, I told you I was having this side-track problem." Abigail was impervious to criticism in much the same way that her trust fund had sailed through the high-tech collapse without a hiccup. "So, have you managed to secure the contract?"

Shelley shifted the phone to her other hand. "It's more like I've made direct contact."

"Meaning that you've met the count?" Abigail's firm voice was more declaratory than anything.

Shelley sighed. "I have, but he's not predisposed to renew the contract for various financial reasons. Though I *have* gotten him to agree to continue the discussions today."

Shelley could practically hear Abigail nodding at the other end of the phone. "Good. And what about Lionel? Don't forget to let him know what the situation is."

"I've already talked to him."

"Excellent. I told you you'd be good at this—with my help, naturally."

Shelley held the phone away and stuck her tongue out at it. When she brought it back to her ear, Abigail was already in midsentence. "Sorry? I missed that part."

"I was saying that when you go to pitch your ideas, just make sure to use a PowerPoint presentation. Nothing impresses the client more than a visual aid—especially one with pie charts."

"I'll keep that in mind." The thought of pie charts made Shelley think of Isabelle's blackberry tart…and Edmond's blue eyes…and her naked foot.

There was a good chance that further sleep wasn't possible.

EDMOND PUNCHED IN THE NUMBER on his cell phone and stared over the stone wall of the garden. In the morning sunlight, the blossoms of the almond trees sparkled like fairy lights, their gaiety a striking contrast to the regimented rows of gnarled grapevines that lay beyond.

His legacy.

His lodestone.

He cursed silently and glanced at his watch. It was a little past nine o'clock—nine-oh-seven, to be exact. Edmond liked being exact. He liked knowing precisely where everything was, what everyone was doing.

Take Vincent, his assistant. Edmond knew that at any moment Vincent would arrive in the office. Fortified by two cups of espresso and a half a pack of Gauloises, he would be ready for a full day's work before heading off at seven o'clock to the Left Bank, where he would consummate his midweek tryst with a shop girl from the Salamander shoe store on Saint Germain-des-Prés.

Thoughts of sex had Edmond searching for his own cigarette lighter. He still found that rubbing the cool metal surface helped him think. It didn't make him stop thinking about Shelley McCleery.

Ever since her arrival, he'd been feeling uncharacteristically on edge. And that preposterous lie of his aunts' that he was a toothpaste salesman hadn't helped matters. Only Shelley's apparent embarrassment at finding the whole thing so absurd had saved him. He hoped.

In fact, he counted on it if he was going to get to the bottom of the theft—the theft of the Montfort Botticelli.

Five days ago, he had returned to the chateau for his stepgrandmother's funeral and made a startling discovery upon wandering through the gallery. The Botticelli, the drawing that his family had always valued so much, was a fake. At some time since he'd last visited—roughly three months ago—the genuine article had been switched for a copy. He knew it as certainly as any Frenchman knows the thirty vacation days he is entitled to take each year.

Edmond had immediately suspected Françoise, and indeed he'd found correspondence to dealers in Paris and Bordeaux in which she'd inquired about selling it. But she had only just started the courtship process.

That his aunts had made the substitution was out of the question. They would have considered it sacrilegious to part with anything to do with the Montfort legacy. For that reason alone, besides not wanting to needlessly alarm them—they were not young, after all—he'd held off telling them.

Now as he waited for Vincent to pick up, he hoped he was getting closer to delivering good news instead of bad.

"J'écoute." I'm listening. At last, Vincent's raspy voice answered from the other end of the line. "Must you always call so early in the morning?"

Edmond didn't bother to apologize. "So, have you found out anything else about *Mademoiselle* Mc-Cleery?" He found himself holding his breath.

"Let's see. Born and raised in northern New York state in a town called She— Sheen—" He ended up spelling *Schenectady*. "Parents divorced. Father originally an insurance salesman, later something called a 'barker' in the circus."

"A shill," Edmond clarified.

"That would fit the other information from court records regarding chronic delinquency of alimony payments. Seems the marriage dissolved about the same time hubby decided to stop selling annuities."

"They were better off without him," Edmond scoffed.

"Well, not necessarily financially. The mother's only income was her salary as a high school English teacher. And there were three children to support. Full Christian names in reverse order, Mary Shelley, Emily Brontë and—"

"Let me guess—Jane Austen."

"Why, yes!" came Vincent's surprised response. "How did you know?"

"It's not important." Edmond didn't think a discussion of English women writers was strictly necessary in cracking this case. "What *is* important is that a childhood history of abandonment and financial insecurity could provide a motive, besides explaining *Mademoiselle* McCleery's high level of practical competence and low-key appearance verging on primness."

Edmond pictured the way Shelley's hair had sprung free from the tortoiseshell barrette. Perhaps *primness* was not quite the right word. Nevertheless, he didn't feel the need to clarify. "Go on," he said. "And did you manage to find out what I asked earlier? The reason for her dropping out of school? Was it poor grades? A scandal?"

"No, nothing outstanding. Apparently, she was disillusioned with academia. Since that time, almost four years ago, she's been with Dream Villas, earning—" there was a pause and a shuffling of papers "—even less than I make." Vincent's voice conveyed real amazement.

"Is she in debt?" Edmond asked.

"No more than usual. She makes partial payments on her Visa bill, probably more to do with her meager salary than an extravagant lifestyle—though she does have a weakness for this place called Victoria's Secret."

Edmond rubbed his upper lip. "Living arrangements?"

"From what our sources say, she was living with a doctor until about nine months ago. But that relationship appears to have dissolved."

"Perhaps she was despondent over the breakup? That, coupled with a history of financial insecurity, could have driven her to crime." Edmond found himself wondering what kind of man Shelley McCleery would live with.

There was silence from the other end of the phone.

Edmond refocused on that. "You don't agree? You think she is innocent?"

Vincent coughed his smoker's cough. At the same time, Edmond could hear him light up yet another cigarette. "I'm not saying she's innocent. It's just, there's the matter of when the Botticelli disappeared. *Mademoiselle* McCleery was nowhere near the chateau as best as we can make out. So maybe her arrival now has nothing to do with the theft? Maybe she really *is* there to renegotiate the contract, as she claims?"

This time the silence came from Edmond's end of the line.

"Boss, what do you think?"

Edmond stopped his pacing. "I think it's time I upped the ante and took her into the cave. As Shakespeare wrote, 'The instruments of darkness tell us truths.'" He recited the line from *Macbeth* in English, the way he'd memorized it from the Moroccan-leather edition his grandfather had given him on his fourteenth birthday.

"*Eh bien*, you can keep your Shakespeare. What I want to know is will this flush out *Mademoiselle* McCleery and solve this case?"

Edmond glanced toward the chateau, to the location of Shelley's bedroom windows. "I'm not sure, not sure at all."

8

SHELLEY FOUND EDMOND IN THE garden, near the wall, bent over the burbling fountain. It was multitiered with a sculpture of a leaping carp poised at the top. A steady stream of water spouted from its open mouth. "Looking for fish?" she asked, peering around his shoulder.

Edmond straightened up. For a man who made an art form out of sophisticated nonchalance, he was surprisingly anxious. "As a matter of fact, I was looking for coins."

Shelley rested her hands on the rim of the basin and shifted her gaze from the pool of water to his face. "Desperate times calling for desperate measures and all that?"

Not that he looked desperate in her estimation. True, the collar of his polo shirt was unraveling in the back and the bands at the short sleeves had the stretched-out, tired look of too many encounters with a French washing machine—one that worked, that is. But the material and cut were unmistakably of the finest quality.

"No, I haven't reached that point—yet." He

smiled slowly and turned sideways, resting his hip against the edge of the fountain's basin. "I was wondering if any of the coins I used to throw for good luck when I was young were still here."

Shelley glanced back. "Doesn't look like it. We could throw more in if you'd like?"

"No, it's not necessary. Anyway, I don't believe in luck anymore."

"Well, I do." Shelley figured that if she didn't have luck, there was no way she was going to get through this latest fiasco. "Too bad I don't have my purse with me now or I'd have tossed in some change."

Edmond reached into his pocket and produced a one-euro coin. "Please, be my guest—which I suppose you are already."

Shelley smiled. "That's too much." He pushed it toward her despite her objection. "Oh, okay. But I have to tell you—I feel completely wicked. As a kid, we never had pennies, let alone the equivalent of a whole euro to throw away." She stood with her back to the fountain, closed her eyes and tossed the coin over her shoulder. It plopped and settled at the bottom of the water.

"So, are you going to tell me?"

She turned and saw him staring at her in that penetrating way of his. "Tell you what?" she asked, wishing—ridiculous, really, given the circumstances—that she'd dressed with more of an eye to her appearance than practicality. Since she'd planned on doing household repairs, she'd worn khakis and a Ralph Lauren boatneck striped shirt—the one she'd gotten for sixty-five cents at the Goodwill shop.

"Tell me what you wished for," he answered and cocked his head, waiting.

"Oh, I couldn't possibly tell. If you do, your wish won't come true." Especially wardrobe wishes.

He turned up one corner of his mouth. "We couldn't have that. I'll change to a safer topic of conversation then. You slept well, I trust? Dreamed pleasant dreams?"

Shelley wasn't sure if that was a safer topic, given last night's imagined lovemaking. She noticed he was watching her carefully, which made her wonder if clairvoyance was one of those traits like hemophilia that was passed down through royal bloodlines. *Nonsense.*

"I slept soundly, thank you." She thrust her hands in her pants pockets. "The bed, as I'm sure you know, is very comfortable. As is everything else. In fact—" she leaned forward from her hips "—do you mind if I tell you a deep, dark secret?"

Edmond leaned toward her, as well. "I would be disappointed if you didn't."

"Well, it probably sounds silly to you—after all, you're used to having Roman statues in your bedroom—but I've always yearned to be surrounded by beautiful old things, felt that it was the type of atmosphere that would make me the most happy. Not the costliness of the objects, exactly, as much as the Old World aesthetic. And don't laugh, but when I first took the job with Dream Villas, I thought I would be staying in places just like this and all over Europe. Was I ever naive!"

The corners of Edmond's lips twitched up, but he wasn't laughing. "And that has made you disgruntled with your job?"

"Let's just say that recently I've come to realize just how dissatisfied I am with my life in general."

"And that has caused you to do some things you'd never contemplated doing before?"

Maybe clairvoyance was part of his genes? Or maybe she had finally met a sensitive male who, given all appearances, was decidedly heterosexual. "Well, I *have* come to some decisions." She cleared her throat. "And I *have* thought of a solution, which I think should be mutually beneficial for both you and me—if you'd like to hear it?"

"I'm all ears." Edmond settled more solidly against the fountain. He gave every indication of being nobly befuddled and utterly relaxed. "And you worked this solution out with *Monsieur* Toynbee?"

"No, it's all my own. I *am* capable of acting independently. I don't always need to run what I do by him," she proclaimed. The new Shelley McCleery was bold, forthright, a virtual superheroine of the luxury vacation-rental business—her khakis and T-shirt being a convenient cover, of course.

Edmond raised an eyebrow in keen anticipation.

"What about bequeathing the chateau to a university, the way Bernard Berenson donated his villa on Lake Como to Harvard?" she suggested. "Scholars, a few at a time, could use the chateau as a retreat,

and you could still hold on to the outer buildings.
That way you'd take the bulk of the estate off the tax
books but continue to have a residence for your
aunts. You'd also have the satisfaction of knowing
that your inheritance, while out of your hands,
would still maintain a certain intellectual dignity."

Edmond stepped away from the fountain. "I'm
sorry, what are you talking about?"

"A way for you to retain the chateau and be able
to renew the leasing agreement with Dream Villas."
Shelley was bewildered. "What did you think I was
talking about?"

Edmond rubbed his chin. "I've had a lot of things
on my mind. I was confused." *To say the least.* From
the tone of the conversation, he'd anticipated that
she was about to confess to stealing the Botticelli.

He dropped his hand to his side and regrouped.
"It's not a bad idea. One I actually thought of. Naturally it would appeal to my aunts, the academic nature
and all. But unfortunately the lawyer informed me
that any such arrangement would have to have been
worked out *before* the *comtesse* passed away."

"Then did you ever consider selling off the chateau for a corporate conference center?" She saw him
frown. "No, I suppose Isabelle and Marie-Jeanne
would have trouble with a lot of strangers milling
about with PalmPilots."

Shelley squeezed her shoulders together in
thought. "You know there's one other obvious answer." She looked up brightly. "I was reluctant to bring
it up, but what about selling off some of the contents?"

Edmond very deliberately leaned back against the fountain. He rested his hands on either side and strummed his fingers on the rim. It was funny, but he had somehow wanted to believe that Shelley Mc-Cleery wasn't mixed up in all this mess. That her freshness and wonder were signs of genuine joy and appreciation.

"It seems you have thought of everything!" he exclaimed, adding a careless smile—the same one that invariably yielded panting invitations to many a bedroom.

Shelley frowned.

Had the smile been too much?

"Well, it's not like I needed to be a rocket scientist to come up with it. I'm sure the thought occurred to you, too?"

"I can't say it didn't, but—"

"I know. I understand," Shelley interrupted him "You probably are reluctant to part with pieces of a guarded legacy. Your aunts explained the notion to me, and I applaud it. Really, I do. It's noble in the true sense of the word. But if it's a question of having to forgo everything you hold near and dear versus giving up a few valuable pieces here and there…"

Edmund gripped the rim of the fountain. "I suppose you're referring to the prized Botticelli drawing in particular?" He kept his tone neutral.

"Yes, there is the Botticelli, and I'm sure it's worth something." Shelley frowned. Hmm. How to put this gently? She knew how much the family cherished the drawing, and it was true that she'd only seen it briefly *and* in poor light, but the truth of the matter was she just didn't think it was all that good.

So how best to put it gently? She shook her head. Probably best not to at all.

Instead she offered a brave smile, and with the marked enthusiasm of an airline hostess demonstrating how to use a life jacket, she said, "But I think you might also want to consider other important holdings. If I'm not mistaken, there's a Gutenberg bible in the library which should do very well at auction. Then there's the medieval ivory in the gallery. You can hardly see it because it's practically hidden, but it's exquisite, and these days medieval minor art has really risen in desirability in Europe, especially France."

"Which is good, because France has strict regulations about taking art out of the country." Edmond drew his lips together. He'd seen the way she'd avoided discussing the Botticelli. Perhaps she meant to keep that for herself while sharing the rest of the wealth, so to speak.

He nodded slowly, formulating his own plan. "You know, I think there's real merit in what you've suggested. Let me just think about it a little more."

Shelley smiled. Maybe, just maybe, there was a light at the end of the tunnel.

"In the meantime, speaking of family treasures, I have one other related idea of my own."

She raised her eyebrows. "Really? What is it?"

"It requires a bit of a walk—to the cave." He paused. "If you're up for it, that is?" He waited for her reaction.

Shelley looked down at her watch and tapped the face. "I would really like to, but I've already set up an appointment with the repairman to fix the washing machine, and it was actually scheduled for fifteen minutes ago. I realize it may seem trivial to you, but with the Nosenbergers coming shortly, I really can't let things slide." She also wanted to let the aunts know as quickly as possible about this latest development and get them to help her persuade Edmond to sell some of the family's valuables. It was probably the only way to solve their problem.

Edmond sensed her reluctance. It made him press harder. "It is highly unlikely for a repairman to arrive within an hour and fifteen minutes of an appointment." He placed his hand under her elbow to guide her.

Shelley stiffened.

"Unless you're afraid of the dark? I promise, I'll be right next to you every step of the way."

"It's not the dark. Other things maybe, but not the dark."

"In which case, shall we conquer our fears together?" And he gave a little tug.

LIONEL ADJUSTED THE KNOT IN his ascot. It was one of his favorites—a pale peach paisley that he had gotten at Thomas Pink in London. The color made him look fetchingly youthful, he thought.

Of course in his youth he would have considered wearing an ascot an effete affectation—not that he'd have known the meaning of either term. What he did know was that he wanted the good life, the kind of life that his greengrocer father couldn't even begin to provide. And that he, Lionel—named Louie back then—was going to have to get it all on his own.

It wouldn't be through good grades—that was for sure. He had a closer familiarity with the principal's office than with any of his textbooks. The preamble to the Constitution, the atomic masses of the elements and Pythagorean theorem—all the details of schooling—didn't interest him.

Instead he'd concentrated on another lesson—the art of charming older women, seducing them, all the while gracefully submitting to their ministrations and financially profitable attention.

Once, when his father had made a home delivery of two melons, a head of Romaine lettuce and five pounds of plum tomatoes to Mrs. Antonelli, he'd found the widow *with* his son—who was *without* his pants. "You skinny-necked kid!" his old man had shouted as he'd dragged Lionel out the door by his ear. "Don't you know you'll never amount to anything if you don't start doing some honest work?"

"We-ell, look who had the la-ast laugh!" For thirty years or so, Lionel's unique talents had provided a means to the end he had always dreamed of.

He removed the Tiffany key ring from his trouser pocket and unlocked his bottom desk drawer. "There you are, my lovelies."

Arranged by color and carefully packed in tissue paper was a large assortment of ascots. About certain things Lionel was careful. Never again would anyone accuse him of having a long, skinny neck.

And he contemplated his upcoming plans. "Something subtle is definitely called for. A gray-on-gray check?" He reached in the middle of the pile but hesitated. "No, understatement is always better. A solid, yes, solid gray."

He pulled out just the one he wanted and stroked the fine silk, feeling his heart rate gradually lower. He had been under so much stress lately, he'd even left the house the other day with mismatched socks.

To think that all he had worked for could go up in smoke! No, he wouldn't let that happen. He'd already put things into motion, sending Shelley to the chateau, following up on the phone.

"She'll do just what's necessary," he said out loud, reassuringly. "Always reli-iable, that girl." He thought a moment. "But it doesn't hurt to have a little extra help."

He looked at the ascot he'd chosen. "Yes, you're definitely the one. But perhaps...?" He let his eyes drift downward to the open drawer. He reached in beneath the ascots and removed a small, rectangular wooden case.

"Yes, it's definitely time to pu-ull out the big guns," he said gravely and lifted the lid.

9

EDMOND GUIDED SHELLEY ALONG the path on the outside of the garden wall. It wound its way up the side of the hill out of view from the chateau. The undergrowth was thick, and instead of steps, they climbed on well-worn rocks that dotted the arid soil. The Yellow Brick Road, it wasn't.

After a series of twists and turns, the path opened up, and several yards to the left a shoulder-high opening cut into the side of the hill. Edmond took Shelley's hand. "Watch your head," he warned. He flicked on the flashlight that he'd retrieved from the kitchen.

They navigated the curving tunnel, and the sunlight from the outside soon disappeared, plunging them into darkness and dropping the temperature ten degrees. Edmond shifted the beam of light upward and stopped.

Shelley, whose head was raised to follow the light, bumped into his shoulder. "Oh, sorry." She pushed away from his side, trying to ignore the solidness of his body. "Talk about making a statement. I have new respect for the power of slowly dripping water."

A massive stalactite hung from the ceiling. It resembled an icicle on steroids and under the glare of the flashlight gave off an opalescent sheen.

Edmond shifted the light to catch her face. She blinked, then waved her hand around. "And this has something to do with your idea for saving the chateau?"

He studied her in that quiet way of his, finally tweaking up the corner of his mouth. "Why don't we look farther? I'm sure it will come to you shortly." He took her hand, and Shelley momentarily flinched. She really wasn't good at this bodily contact thing. But Edmond squeezed her fingers reassuringly, and she relaxed—well, enough to put one foot in front of the other.

The passageway curved to the right and after a short decline opened up into a second open space. Edmond directed the beam around, illuminating a giant cluster of spires thrusting upward and downward, filling the ceiling and most of the floor space.

He started to walk on, but Shelley held him back. "Wait. Not so fast. I think I'm catching on. Your idea? For the cave? You want to turn it into a tourist attraction, kind of the way we're exploring it, only with handrails and eco-friendly sources of power. I'm right, aren't I?"

Actually, no. But he'd play along. "You mean we can't have gaudy colored lights and tacky names? And here I was hoping to call the first large stalactite Santa Claus."

Shelley frowned, not realizing it was a joke.

"Maybe you're right. No Las Vegas show lights—this is a tasteful operation the whole way—but the tacky names do have entertainment value. Though for the first one I think I prefer Old Faithful." She saw he didn't quite get the reference. "The geyser at Yellowstone National Park?"

He extended his jaw and nodded.

"And the chamber here, something like the Organ Pipes, or even better—" she counted with her finger "—yes, I thought so. Snow White and the Seven Dwarfs."

She sounded remarkably sincere. "Just like Snow White," he echoed.

Shelley looked at Edmond. He didn't appear to be eyeing her with the Disney cartoon in mind.

And he wasn't. Because Edmond was trying to decide if Shelley McCleery was either as genuinely innocent as she seemed or very, very good at her con game. In the meantime, he would just play along. "And you really think this idea of turning the cave into a tourist attraction has merit?"

"In the long term, definitely," Shelley replied. "But there are the up-front costs and time necessary to build a proper walkway, install lighting, get insurance and of course set up the all-important gift shop."

"You mean the tax men are not going to wait until we reap the profits from the first million T-shirts?"

"P-le-ease, spare me the drama." What she could tell him about the tax men! Still, if she held one truth to be self-evident, besides the fact that good shoes and a fine handbag made any outfit, you didn't get through life by hiding your head in the sand—or retreating to the greenhouse like her mother. You had to face problems head-on!

"Listen, I think we should consider transforming the cave as a solution for down the line—" Shelley used a chopping hand motion to emphasize her point "—but in the short term we need to focus on selling a portion of the Montfort art collection as a way to preserve the bulk of your family's heritage."

"Always on the lookout for safeguarding my family's good name?" Again, he vacillated between his appreciation of her sincerity and his disgust for her charade. His instincts told him not to trust her, but something else—his heart? no, couldn't be—wanted to believe in her genuineness.

"I would have thought that you more than anyone would want to ensure the memory of your family, especially those who've passed away?" she asked. Wasn't that what honoring a legacy was all about?

Edmond narrowed his eyes, and this time, his stare didn't focus on anything in the cave. "My memories of those who've died? Frankly, the only thing that stands out is seeing my parents and my grandmother run over that day. Even though it was so many years ago, I can still recall how amazingly sunny it was, absolutely perfect, just what people imagine the weather to be when they think of the Riviera."

He saw her horrified look. "Yes, I was there when they were killed. The only reason I was saved was that I'd stopped a few paces back to tie my shoelace.

It had come undone, you see. And I remember that vividly because my mother had insisted I wear these rather formal dress shoes. So I bent over and was doing up the knot—" he unconsciously mimicked the motion "—then looking up…" His voice drifted off.

He shook his head. "But you know, the really awful part is not so much remembering that day as *not* remembering other days. Because as much as I loved my parents, and I adored them as a child—they were so glamorous, so devoted to each other—I find that as time goes on, I almost can't picture them anymore. And that's the tragic part. It's like I've lost them twice, once for real, the second in my memories. And losing the chateau will make their memories slip away even more completely."

Shelley felt his sadness. Felt for once he wasn't using lofty sarcasm as a means to separate and protect himself from the world. She had to do something, needed to heal his hurt, show him that he wasn't so alone.

She raised her hand and brushed her fingertips across his lower lip. He peered down. There was silence except for the distant, muted thrum of running water and the nearer, louder sound of her breathing. And his.

And then she went up on the toes of her sneakers, wrapped her hand around his neck and kissed him.

Edmond brought his hands to her shoulders and his lips more firmly to her mouth. The flashlight skittered to the floor, plunging them in darkness.

And Shelley knew she wasn't in Philadelphia anymore. Knew that her lips had never received so intimate an exploration, in a way that made them feel plump and ripe like a Jersey peach left out on a hot August day. Knew that the roof of her mouth had never tingled with such an intensity, even after consuming a whole bag of SweeTARTS her first year at summer camp.

Knew beyond the shadow of a doubt that the man with whom she was locked in an embrace was no novice at this kissing business. Yet for all his savoir faire, she could feel that he was shaking every bit as much as she.

A revelation that surprised him, too. Not that Edmond hadn't thought about kissing her for a while. A while? Ever since he'd laid eyes on her that first day and watched her, her eyes closed, lazing in the sun like a cat—only to open them and reveal green irises that were at once dazzling and skittish.

And as his tongue tasted the sweet ridges of the roof of her mouth while his hands dived through her thick hair, loosening it from that maddening pin she insisted on wearing, he felt his longing grow. Didn't she realize that by disciplining that mass of curls she was begging a man to free it?

He was supposed to be wrestling with whether Shelley McCleery was guilty or innocent, not succumbing to contact. Not that he was in any hurry to break contact. Forget his suspicions about her and his agony about his own financial woes. My God, his memories of Jersey girls were good but not this good!

He slipped his hand under the hem of her top and caressed her stomach. Her skin was soft and warm, and he could feel the outline of her ribs and the smoothness of her muscles. He moved his fingers higher and felt the netlike material of her bra. The clasp came undone in a matter of moments, and he heard her gasp as he spread his fingers, taking the weight of her breast. Then he brought his thumb and middle finger together and pinched her nipple.

She let out a strangled cry.

And he groaned—at the immediate response of her body *and* at the realization of just what he was doing. *Mon Dieu*, he was in the middle of an investigation! An investigation to salvage something of his family's legacy, not to mention his pride.

Edmond abruptly pulled his hand back. "We can't do this."

His words jolted her like a double espresso with a heaping spoonful of superfine sugar. Shelley blinked to clear her head and worked frantically to collect herself—not easy with her bra hanging from her elbows. *Oh, crap!* She'd offered the kiss as an act of comfort. And it had quickly, unexpectedly, escalated—combusted—into something far more dangerous.

She should have remembered that Edmond de Montfort was out of her league. Reminded herself that she couldn't afford to jeopardize her mission to secure the contract renewal.

"You're right," she said, attempting to recover from the disaster, not knowing if it were even possible. "It's entirely unprofessional of me." Shelley shimmied up her bra straps and turned around, fastening the hook and adjusting the necessary body parts to achieve a reasonable sense of decorum. Then she smoothed her hair back. Where was her barrette? *Oh, forget it.* She yanked a lock behind one ear and shifted around to face him again.

He was bending down to pick up the flashlight, and the beam of light caught an image on the wall.

"Hold on. What…what's that?" She reached out, her fingers hovering over but not quite touching the dark, dank surface.

There against the wall blackened by soot from a fire was the outline of five fingers and a palm.

"It's a handprint from seventy-five thousand years ago, the Paleolithic Age." How much easier to play tour guide than confront what had just transpired.

Shelley spread her fingers and held her hand next to the print. They were approximately the same size. "You mean…?"

"That someone left his mark here in times long past. And he also drew this." Edmond stepped to the side and shone the light higher. "If you look closely, you can see the faint outlines of a horse." He let the light follow the contours of the primitive picture formed by bold black and red lines. "There's the flank, its back and then the head and the snout."

"This is amazing. I knew there were cave paintings in France and Spain, but to see them in person is just, just…" She stared, awestruck. She felt as if Edmond had just opened up a new world to her—a world of wonder and mystery.

No, get real, girl. Their kiss had already opened up *that* world. The sight of the cave painting only reinforced it. Too much time spent around Edmond de Montfort, especially in close quarters, took her beyond everything that was familiar. Everything that she felt capable of controlling.

"Come. Let's go to the next chamber. There's another drawing in particular that I want you to see." He was intent on getting his investigation back on track. And right now, the depths of the cave held the key.

"No, I don't think so." Shelley shook her head. She couldn't risk making a further fool of herself. Maddening as it was, she could still feel the effects of his kiss on her lips. And still realized that where Edmond de Montfort was concerned, she seemed to have no control at all. "I don't think that would be a good idea."

"And why is that?"

Shelley stood up straight. "You and I both know why. I've already done something I regret. I'm very sorry it happened and at the same time I don't want to risk compounding the damage. I'd like you to hold off judging me until I've had a chance to try to make amends."

Edmond arched one brow. So, he had been correct in suspecting her honesty? There no longer seemed to be any question about it, despite the benefit of the doubt he may have wanted to give her.

Still, what he needed was hard evidence. And if

going farther into the cave was not an immediate option, he had another idea about where to look. "All right," he agreed, speaking slowly. "But we *will* resolve this at some point, you know?"

Shelley held her breath and nodded once.

"In the meantime, why don't I take you back? I know you mentioned taking care of some repairs—with my aunts, I presume?"

"Yes." Shelley nodded. "Won't you be joining us?"

"No, I need to take care of some work, but don't worry, you shall see me. In fact, you won't be able to get rid of me."

"IS SHE NOT WONDERFUL!" Isabelle exclaimed. "To think, she is able to bring light where once there was darkness."

"I think you may be exaggerating a tad." Shelley was crouched on the floor. She seemed to be doing a lot of that since meeting the aunts. "It's just a plug, and as you can see, all that was necessary were wire cutters and a quick trip to Mr. Bricolage," she said, referring to the Home Depot of France.

"Still, your triumph is nothing less than what I have come to expect." Marie-Jeanne crossed off the item from her list with gusto. "Your ability to resolve problems rivals Sam Spade's finesse at solving cases." She had just elevated Shelley to the pantheon of Raymond Chandler immortals.

"*C'est elle qui peut la mieux vous aider—et moi.*" *She's the best person to help you—and me,* Marius, the chateau's gardener and not-so-competent jack-of-all-trades, announced triumphantly. Shelley and Marius had communicated via letters or telephone, but this was their first face-to-face encounter. Over the course of their long-distance relationship, spurred on by several malfunctioning toilets and cracked window casements, he had relayed his many sorrows: his wife Claudine's desertion more than thirty years ago with a shoe salesman from Lyons; his son's firing from his position as a doorman at the Plaza Athénée in Paris and subsequent decision to join a reggae band—the latter more horrifying than the former.

Shelley had at long last grasped the fact that the sixty-year-old workman had an enormous crush on her. That he wasn't now communicating his fervor more forcefully was due to the moderating presence of his aristocratic employers as well as Shelley's difficulty in understanding his strong Provençal accent. That he was missing his two top front teeth marred his amorous outpourings also.

Shelley stood up. "What's next?" She peered over Marie-Jeanne's shoulder at the neat copperplate column of overdue repairs.

Marie-Jeanne held the embossed leather notebook at arm's length. Vanity kept her from purchasing reading glasses. "The damage to the plaster in the gallery."

Shelley thought a moment. "Maybe we can wait until after we check on how the washing machine repairman is doing?" She wasn't sure which she was less willing to tackle.

She supposed she should have been overjoyed when the local Miele dealership—as soon as they found out it was *Mademoiselle* McCleery from "Phee-lee-del-phia"—had promised to send a repairman the very same day. The dust in the driveway still hadn't settled from the van's arrival.

Toto, the appliance repairman, had performed miracles on earlier occasions with the vacuum cleaner and the refrigerator/freezer. Now, upon disgorging his wiry frame from the front seat, he had beheld Shelley—with her hair still loose from the cave and grown even wilder after snaking the blocked-up toilet in the ground-floor powder room—and declared, *"Vous êtes Juliette à mon Romeo." You are Juliet to my Romeo.* Actually he hadn't so much declared it as turned it into a three-minute aria. Apparently, Toto had a thing for Gounod's operas, especially *Romeo et Juliette*, in addition to electrical appliances.

It was all Shelley had needed.

"Perhaps, Marius, you could check with Toto first to see if he is ready for us?" She had no desire to face the flamboyant repairman anytime soon. Besides, she needed time alone with the aunts.

Shelley waited for Marius to leave and turned to Isabelle and Marie-Jeanne. "I wanted to speak to you privately about renewing the agreement with Dream Villas."

"Yes, we have been anxious to bring it up, as well," Marie-Jeanne confided. "The thought of having to leave our home weighs on us heavily. It has been hard not to show our distress to Edmond."

"Have you managed to convince him then? About the contract?" Isabelle asked. The two huddled around her closely, like couture-clad covered wagons circling the fire.

"Not exactly. I have made some progress, but I could definitely use your help. I realize you may find the idea initially abhorrent, but if Edmond were willing to sell some of the family's artwork or rare volumes from the library, there might be enough money to clear the debts."

"Part with the Montfort legacy!" Marie-Jeanne was aghast.

"Would you rather see the whole estate—including the treasures—fall into other hands? But if the count were to part with a few choice items—and I emphasize *a few*—he could save the chateau and pass it on to his children and their children to come."

"Oh, to think of the possibility of children!" Isabelle clasped her ring, then shook her head in a moment of seeming clarity. "My ring? Surely it could be of some value? I could give it to you now." She vainly tried to work it over her knuckle.

Shelley rested her hand on the old woman's. "That's not necessary. I'm sure that some of your items could help to raise money, but it need not be anything so personal. In any case, the auction price of some of the art pieces far exceeds the value of your ring."

Isabelle smiled with relief, the creases in her cheeks loosening some of her custom-made powder.

Marie-Jeanne nodded smartly. "As usual, you are right, Shel-lee. We will of course try to persuade Edmond that he would be doing the right thing and that he would have our support."

"Good. I knew I could rely on you." She looked up when she heard Marius come back into the study.

"Zee man, Toto. He wishes to speak to you," he said. "But I will follow." He puffed out his chest. "To make sure he is doing the right thing."

"Fine." Shelley wasn't about to get in the way of dueling repairmen. She beat a path to the laundry room with the aunts and Marius in tow. She just hoped the Nosenbergers appreciated the lengths she had to go to assure their harmonious stay.

Once she entered the laundry room, she saw the heel of one work boot sticking out behind the washer. *"Est-ce que vous avez trouvé la problème?" Have you found the problem?* Shelley circled around the appliance.

Toto was on his knees, his toolbox open and its contents dispersed on the tiles. "I am grieved to inform you that someone has tampered with the machine." His voice was sorrowful.

"Someone's tried to damage it?" Shelley was alarmed.

"Perhaps someone misguidedly tried to fix it himself?" Toto critically eyeballed Marius.

Marius held up his hands. "I swear. I didn't go anywhere near it." He recognized someone younger and fitter than he.

Shelley glanced at Marius, taking in his sincerity and knowing his innate phlegmatic personality. She doubted he had attempted to make the repairs. Perhaps one of the women in to clean for the funeral had tried her hand and failed, afraid to tell anyone. Whatever. It wasn't important now.

"Does that mean that to fix it is not covered under the warranty?" Marie-Jeanne's syntax may be all over the map, but the 'gist of her concern was transparent.

"I am afraid, *madame*, that if unauthorized personnel have tampered with the appliance, the company cannot assume the burden of the costs." Toto held up his hand as if swearing the Miele oath.

Shelley pictured a stupendous repair bill and the subsequent loss of faith by the two aunts in her abilities, leading, in turn, to the inevitable failure to renew the contract.

No, that simply was *not* going to happen.

"Toto," she said sweetly, touching his shoulder in the most virginal way possible. She had a feeling that this might appeal to his image of her as Juliet. "Isn't it possible that the washer was originally damaged when it was delivered from the factory, and with use, it finally broke down fully?" She batted her eyelashes and sighed. "It would destroy me—" she placed her hand dramatically on her chest and heaved her bosom, or as much as one can heave 34Bs "—to think that the repair wasn't covered."

Toto's jaw dropped, revealing his yellowed teeth. Edmond's full product range of peroxide-gel toothpaste, dental rinse and whitening strips had a prime candidate in the making. "I could not have that on my conscience, *mademoiselle*." He slowly raised his outstretched hand to head level—Pavarotti couldn't have done it better—and announced, "For you, I will make an exception."

Isabelle stopped furiously turning her moonstone ring.

Marie-Jeanne summarily crossed off another item on the list.

And Marius appeared to stew a moment before announcing, "And I will feed the geraniums without you having to remind me, *Mademoiselle* Sheell-eey."

At which point, Shelley turned, looked out the window of the laundry room, and smiled to herself. She could handle this in-person stuff after all. Maybe she, and everyone else for that matter, was seeing the birth of a new Shelley McCleery, one who *could* actually work miracles.

Then she remembered there was someone missing from this triumph in cost-free appliance repair. Was he in denial about his responsibilities regarding the chateau or temporarily avoiding her after what had happened in the cave? She wasn't sure which was more troubling.

One thing for sure. There was still someone yet to be won over.

10

EDMOND CLOSED THE DOOR BEHIND him and took in the contents of the room in one sweeping glance. His childhood bedroom was evocative of good times and bad. But it had always been his—until now.

One thing was sure about Shelley McCleery—she was a tidy person. Her closed suitcase sat squarely on the luggage rack and her extra pairs of shoes were lined up neatly below. He drew his lips together, recognizing with a certain fondness her black slide loafers with the hand stitching.

Never mind the shoes.

He moved to the dresser. Shelley's immaculately clean comb and brush were lined up perfectly straight and lay next to a silver frame with a photo of his mother and him when he was a toddler.

Behind them, vying for space with some of his toy soldiers from the Battle of Waterloo, was a small bottle of Cacharel perfume. He picked it up and brought it to his nose. There was that light, floral, baby-powdery smell that he had already come to associate with Shelley.

He felt his eyes drawn back to the photo on the

dresser. He recognized the pebbly beach at Cap Ferrat, but was more transfixed by his mother. She had her long hair pulled back in a scarf, and large, dark sunglasses dominated her smiling face. Her gold hoop earrings, which glinted in the sun, matched the thin gold leather straps of her sandals. He couldn't remember that day at the beach anymore, but if he closed his eyes and concentrated, he could still smell his mother's perfume—the heady, tropical scent of Ysatis by Givenchy, so different than Shelley's.

He opened his eyes and lowered the perfume bottle. He wasn't here to reminisce. He was here to find evidence of Shelley's guilt.

He swiftly opened the top drawer and found her neatly folded underwear. He wet his lips. Vincent's information was accurate. The lacy bras and panties in vibrant colors bore Victoria's Secret tags. He was mildly embarrassed and was about to close the drawer when he noticed a slim document folder under one pile.

He slipped it out and opened it. Her U.S. passport was brand new, with a less-than-flattering picture and an absence of any immigration stamps. Either she'd used another passport on her previous travels, or she had simply never been out of the country before. He put it down and moved to the remaining contents of the folder: a checkbook and a small address book. He took out both and sat on the edge of the bed—which she'd made—and examined them carefully.

The checkbook showed no large deposits other

than her monthly paycheck, which could never be considered large by any stretch of the imagination. There was a record of payments to cover the usual bills, but as he flipped through the check register, he noticed that she seemed to be highly generous for someone of her limited means. There were numerous donations to various family and children's charities.

He closed the checkbook and turned to the address book. Inside the front cover was a list of birthdays for family and friends. Toynbee's wasn't among them. The phone numbers and addresses on the alphabetized pages appeared to belong to the same people, with the addition of the gas and electric and phone companies.

Edmond rose and replaced the items where he'd found them. Then he checked the rest of the drawers and the closet, finding nothing but neatly organized clothes that were classic designs but nothing expensive. If Shelley McCleery were cashing in on stolen goods, she didn't seem inclined to spend it on finery.

Edmond glanced at his watch. He still had some more time. He crossed over to the suitcase, unsnapped the clips and lifted the lid. And stopped. Inside was a padded carrying case. Holding his breath, he gripped the zipper tab and slowly eased it open. He rounded the last corner, and suddenly conscious that he'd been holding his breath, he forced himself to breathe. Then he gently lifted the top.

And stared. And almost found himself laughing.

Nothing like finding a diaphragm and several packets of condoms.

Edmond rezipped the case and placed it back in the suitcase. Then he ran his hands around the edges and in the side pockets. The only thing he turned up was a tattered old photo. It looked to be Shelley's family, the whole lot of them redheads—the father, still on the scene, included. They were huddled in front of a tent, squinting into the sun and peeling in various stages of sunburn. He recognized Shelley immediately from her forthright chin and the way her hair was pulled back tightly. Already she seemed the only member of the group competently in charge.

Edmond closed the suitcase. So far, the only conclusions he could draw from Shelley's possessions were that she was an orderly person, scrupulous about fulfilling family obligations and practicing safe sex, a soft touch when it came to kids and given to understated tastes in clothing—except when it came to matters of underwear. Hardly the profile of a ruthless international art thief—even the underwear part.

And then Edmond's eyes lighted on her laptop, which sat open on the small writing desk by the window. In for a penny, in for a pound. He tapped the mouse. The screen came to life. He bent down and read the heading at the top: Estimates of Value.

Beneath this, she'd listed various pieces of art from the chateau as well as several first editions, all with monetary values next to them. He skimmed the list and found the Botticelli drawing. Instead of a dollar amount, Shelley had typed in a series of question marks.

He shifted the mouse, tapped it once and minimized the list. Then he glanced at the other items on the desktop. There it was—a file labeled Important Contact Information. Not that he anticipated finding the list of well-known fences, but stranger things had been known to occur.

He opened it and skimmed the contents. It contained phone numbers for herself and Toynbee, but it also included a list of people identified as repairmen in the local area.

He got out his phone and dialed. "Vincent, I need you to check on some names. We may have a lead after all."

FEARFUL THAT TOTO WAS GOING to break into some heart-wrenching aria at any moment, Shelley escaped to the gallery, where in silence she nursed her headache—a result of nonstop conversing in French, she told herself. *Yeah, sure, right.*

She slipped her cell phone out of her pocket. There was no point procrastinating any longer. It was time to phone Lionel for the second time. Okay, she couldn't give him a total thumbs-up, but she could claim forward progress.

She punched in the office number, unconcerned that it would still be very early in the morning. Lionel, after all, kept "Cah-ontinental hours."

The phone rang several times before voice mail kicked in. She hung up. Maybe he was letting the calls go through to the machine so that he could monitor them? She rang again, getting the same result. After the recorded message—her recorded message—finished, she spoke. "Lionel? Lionel? Are you there? It's I, Shelley." Good grammar was important, especially in moments of extreme distress.

He didn't pick up.

She frowned. That was weird. It was one thing to be in denial and it was another to be completely out of touch.

"Answering the phone shouldn't be too challenging, even for someone as technologically inept as you, Lionel," Shelley thought out loud. She disconnected, punched in another number and wandered through the gallery. She stopped with her back to the Botticelli.

"Abigail Braithwaite," came the clipped voice over the phone.

"Abigail, it's Shelley. I haven't called at a bad time, have I?"

"I'm only in the midst of representing a major investment institution which is the defendant in a sex-discrimination suit. This means I'll probably have the top billing hours among the partners for this quarter, but even *I* wonder about the legitimacy of what I'm doing sometimes."

Okay, Shelley figured that now would probably *not* be a good time to confide about the kiss in the cave. "Abigail, you are the very epitome of moral rectitude. I have every confidence that you will do the right thing. Now, I just want to ask—"

"You know, that's what Paul said to me over the phone earlier today. At least, I think that's what he meant. He used what I think was a basketball analogy. Something about spending a good foul versus a bad one?"

Shelley was taken aback, and not just by the fact that Paul had used a metaphor. "You talked to Paul? On the phone?"

"Well, er, yes." Abigail cleared her throat. "That was after we'd had coffee together, which I know is hard to believe—for you as well as for me. But I'll have you know, most of the time we talked about you," Abigail finished with a defensive rush.

"Actually I'd prefer it if you guys talked about other things besides me."

"You're not just saying that?"

Did Shelley detect a hint of insecurity? Whatever. "Of course I'm not. I've got far more pressing problems to deal with. You didn't happen to hear from Lionel, did you?"

"Lionel? No, why on earth would I?"

"Because I gave him your number as an emergency contact in case of, well, in case of any emergency. And since I can't seem to reach him, I thought maybe he called you with a question, like how to turn on the fax machine."

"Knowing Lionel, he's probably forgotten which end of the phone is up. As Paul wisely pointed out—"

Shelley wondered when Paul had suddenly become "wise."

"—the man wouldn't be able to function if he didn't have you in the office to practically wipe his nose."

Shelley didn't want to visualize that image. "Well, I'm still concerned. This *is* our busiest time of year."

"Shelley, I wouldn't worry. Surely Lionel is capable of delaying whatever requests come through until your confident hand returns. Besides, now is not the time for you to worry about things going on back at the office. You need to focus all your energies on the count." Then, almost as an afterthought, she asked, "How is that going, by the way?"

Shelley rubbed her forehead. "There's some progress to report. I offered several suggestions for overcoming his objections to renewing the contract, and one in particular seemed to show real promise. Luckily, I've also managed to get his aunts to work on persuading him. In fact, they insisted that I move in to the chateau."

"It sounds to me like you have the situation well under control. Just think, in addition to the increased opportunity for finalizing the contract, you can have one of the whirlpool baths all to yourself." There was the sound of voices in the background. "Hold on a minute, will you?"

Shelley studied her nails. So far, all the French women she'd seen had these gorgeous manicures, whereas she…

"Shelley, are you still there?" Abigail came back on the line.

Shelley dropped her hand. "Yes?"

"Listen, I really must go. But I just had to ask. It was the PowerPoint presentation that I suggested earlier that tipped the scales, wasn't it?"

Shelley thought of the estimates she'd made for the auction value of some of the items in the Montfort collection, estimates sitting on her laptop and which she'd yet to show Edmond. "You're right. It was the presentation all the way." She disconnected and flipped off the phone.

Then she looked up.

Edmond was right outside one of the gallery's French doors and honing in on her.

"Why am I not surprised to find you here despite the claim of having to do repairs?"

His critical tone wasn't lost on Shelley. She wondered what had brought that on, other than looming insolvency, overwhelming family obligations and a job that seemed to lurch from crisis to crisis.

But after too much—much too much—basso profundo, she had only limited sympathy to spare. "For your information, I've had my nose to the grindstone all day getting this place in order for the Nosenbergers. And as for being here, I was just taking a short break to call the office in Philadelphia—not that that's really a break—and then I was going to have a look at the plaster on the wall. It's peeling." She pointed over her shoulder.

And realized almost simultaneously that venting at the count was probably *not* the best way to win him over. "Not that you need to know the details of the various projects," she said, trying to make amends. "That's my job, as opposed to yours." The details of which still confused her. "In any case, as soon as I finish up here, I was hoping we could grab some time together to continue our negotiations?" She waited for his answer with a tight-lipped smile.

Only one thing she'd said interested him. "And did you get through?"

"Sorry?"

"Did you contact *Monsieur* Toynbee?"

"Actually he didn't pick up. But I'm sure he'll get back to me shortly."

"*Mademoiselle* McCleer-eey. Sheell-eey." A deep voice resonated from the front hall. Toto arrived at the entrance to the gallery. Chest heaving, he rushed in on the parquet floor and dramatically flung himself to his knees. "For you, I have solved the mystery of the motor." He lowered his voice and his chin. "And at no charge." After a brief pause—Shelley wasn't sure but she thought she heard him count *un, deux, trois*—he slowly raised his head and accompanied the beseeching gesture with a long inhalation of breath.

Shelley's headache just cranked up another notch. She stepped back and glanced over at Edmond.

He started to roll his eyes upward but halted when something behind her caught his attention. Not the Botticelli but the fact that the plaster *was* peeling.

"Shell-ee, did you hear the good news?" Marie-Jeanne marched in, notebook in hand. She saw Toto still on his knees, his hand raised in supplication. "Really, young man. On your feet!"

Toto scrambled up, clutching his cap in his hands.

"It works at last!" Isabelle fluttered in next. She stopped when she saw Edmond. "Edmond, did you hear that the washing machine is fixed—and for free? What would we do without our Shell-ee?"

Suddenly it was "our Shelley," he noticed.

"You must have also heard about her wonderful suggestion for the art?" Marie-Jeanne waved her hand around. "It is not as if anyone even enjoys it in this dark and damp room. Truly, you cannot be happy about locking it away like so?"

Actually, Edmond thought but didn't say that if they had been better about locking it away, perhaps the Botticelli wouldn't have up and disappeared.

"That's a good point, Marie-Jeanne." Shelley was pleased to have reinforcements. "If some of the art were to go to a museum, many more people would be able to admire it, and naturally there would be a plaque identifying its origin."

Isabelle put her hands together in prayer. "Did you hear that? The legacy would continue for all to see. For your children and your children's children to come. And it would all be due to you." She blinked her eyes rapidly and shifted her head between Edmond and Shelley.

"Er, yes," Edmond answered haltingly. All this talk of children—his children—was a bit disconcerting.

"Sheell-eey." Marius came running into the room—actually, it was more like a rapid shuffle. "Zee geraniums I have fed. They are beautiful. And all for you." He took a dramatic step in front of Toto.

This time Edmond finished rolling his eyes. It was ridiculous! He couldn't possibly carry out an investigation in the midst of a three-ring circus.

"I think it's time *Mademoiselle* McCleery and I took

a short trip *away* from the chateau." He leveled his most countlike stare.

Shelley breathed a sigh of relief. She was beginning to feel she would never get out from under this entourage she'd somehow acquired, let alone complete her mission. And complete it she would. "That's what I was hoping to hear. Just promise me you won't sing."

"Not to worry—my plan is for you to be the one singing."

11

Les Baux de Provence was tailor-made for picture postcards. It had all the gothic elements of *Wuthering Heights* but without the moors, and all the magic of *The Lord of the Rings* minus the hobbits.

And it was windy as all get out.

Shelley stood along an ancient-looking metal railing. She hoped it was more than just a nod to safety, because besides a strong sense of self-preservation, it was the only thing preventing her from catapulting over the edge of the cliff. The powerful gusts whipped her hair across her face. Behind her lay the ruins of the old citadel and medieval village. In front, the arid, chalky plains dotted with gnarled olive trees. In the distance, Mont Ventoux, adored by painters but cursed by riders in the Tour de France.

She turned around so that the small of her back rested gingerly against the iron railing. "I bet you bring all the girls here."

"Only the ones I want to impress." Edmond joined her by the railing.

"Well, it's pretty impressive all right. Not exactly

beautiful in a soft and fuzzy way but powerful." Shelley pulled a lock of hair out of her mouth.

"The lords who ruled Les Baux would have been delighted to hear that. They were a particularly nasty bunch. In fact, there was even one called the Scourge of Provence. No, I'm not making it up," he answered her look of disbelief. "According to legend, he was supposed to have enjoyed forcing his prisoners to jump off the castle walls." Edmond made a loop-de-loop motion with his hand over the side of the rail.

Shelley followed the downward turn with her eyes. Judging the drop, she thought it was best to step away from the edge. "Relatives of the Monforts, were they?"

Edmond shook his head. His hair blew all over his forehead. On him it looked good. Typical. "On the contrary, the Montforts have always been known as lovers, not fighters."

"Yeah? But I bet you can get just as nasty." She held up her hands in defense. "But only in the nicest possible way."

She found him staring at her in his Edmond-like way—curious, amused and with a hint of something that Shelley was pretty sure was either lust or a close approximation thereof. He took a tentative step toward her. "Why don't we be honest with each other? And I don't mean concerning contracts or works of art. Just you and me. Woman to man."

Shelley gripped the railing behind her. This was dangerous territory. Where was his suggestion going? Was he trying to get at something else?

She didn't know, but she decided the best way to respond was to be completely professional, to treat his proposition like one of those trust-building exercises where a participant is supposed to fall, expecting his partner to catch him.

"All right." She nodded tentatively. "Complete honesty."

"Good." And it was—professional. But also personal. Because no matter how many doubts he had about Shelley McCleery, no matter how great his commitment to solving the case, Edmond also found himself intensely interested in her not as a suspect but as a woman.

"So, tell me then, what do you think of me?" he asked.

Talk about a loaded question. "You sure this isn't going to come back and bite me?" she asked back.

"Only if you're not honest."

Shelley looked over her shoulder at the cliff and decided to take the plunge. *What doesn't kill you makes you stronger.* "Okay, I think you're a fraud." She glanced back at him to see his reaction.

Edmond stiffened. He'd been right. That whole story about being a toothpaste salesman had been too hard to swallow. Still, he didn't panic. "In what way?"

"Like the way you put on this whole supercilious demeanor. Your kind of courtly aloofness. I think it's all a show. I think that deep down you're a pussycat, like Boris Spassky."

Edmond blinked. This is not what he'd been expecting to hear. "I'm afraid you are sadly mistaken—

about Boris. The worthless cat may appear to be affectionate, but he actually employs his guile for one purpose and one purpose only—food." He thought of the way the cat had helped him in the cave and as a reward got one—no, two—tins of sardines.

"There you go again—all sophisticated wit and charm. And anyway, I think you're wrong about the cat," Shelley disagreed. "You underestimate Boris's motives precisely because he wants you to underestimate them. He could go elsewhere to scrounge his food, but does he? No, he patiently allows your aunts their idiosyncrasies precisely because he is so fond of them. And that's just what you do, too."

Shelley held up her hand when she saw he was going to interrupt. "Don't deny it. I mean, look at the prelude to this trip. First, you waited while Isabelle fixed an enormous hamper of food. Tell me, was that completely necessary?"

"Not exactly. There is a country inn down the hill with one of the finest two-star restaurants in all of France."

"But did you remind her of that fact? No-o-o. Because that would have hurt her feelings. You do and say things because you don't want to hurt the ones you love, not to mention lose the ones you love—it's a protection against any future abandonment."

Shelley saw him work his jaw. "I'm sorry, but you asked me to be honest."

Edmond's head shot up. "So I did."

"So?"

"So?" He frowned.

"Now it's your turn to tell me what you think about me. We made a bargain, right?"

"Right." His frown didn't go away. If anything, it deepened. "I'm confused," he answered finally. Honestly.

"Confused?" Shelley pushed her chin back. "I would have thought I'm pretty straightforward?"

"You are—pretty and straightforward," Edmond agreed.

She blushed.

"And that's refreshing."

"You make me sound like a milkmaid."

"Don't downplay your virtues. I admire you for them. Your generosity, your can-do attitude, your sense of humor. It's just…just…"

There was that stare again.

"Just?" Shelley prompted.

Edmond moved in front of her. "It's just that I can't help but wonder about your motives."

"My motives?" She tried not to think about how near he was to her.

"For your visit. You say you're here to renegotiate the contract with Dream Villas, but I find it hard to believe that Dream Villas would be so desperate."

"The chateau *is* one of our most lucrative properties."

"But surely you have others, or are you always on the lookout for new listings? Being dropped by a client can't be a new experience. Why so frantic and why now?"

Shelley swallowed and considered her options. "All right, you really want to know why I'm here?"

He raised one eyebrow.

She swallowed again. "I *could* say that I believe it's important for you to hold on to the estate. That these days everyone wants things that are newer and bigger and faster, at the same time losing sight of the fundamental beauty and grandeur that comes with age, the kind of richness embodied by the Montfort holdings. And I do believe all that, I really do. But I would be lying if I said that would be the only reason I'm intent on securing this deal."

"Go on." He found himself almost dreading to hear her words.

Shelley sniffed. "The truth of the matter is, Dream Villas needs the cash from the summer rental of the chateau. If you don't renew the contract, we'll have to return the rental fee and we'll be in real trouble. Not that I want you to think that Dream Villas is a shoddily run operation. God knows with the work I put into it, it's not. I mean, why would you want to do business with us if we didn't know what we were doing? It's just that this is a onetime snafu. Something Lionel thought he could handle but couldn't."

She searched Edmond's face for his reaction. A small muscle in his cheek twitched. Not a helluva lot to go on.

"He has an urgent debt? Some creditor he needs to pay off?" Edmond asked slowly.

Shelley shrugged. "If only it were that simple. Yes, it's true that Lionel's tailoring bills are chronically overdue *and* enormous, but that's the least of his worries. We're talking about the IRS—the Internal Revenue Service. You see, Dream Villas is under the gun for delinquent back taxes, and we need to make a payment immediately or risk foreclosure."

"Which means you'd lose your job?"

"Among other things." Shelley didn't bother to go into details. "So, there you have it. But I swear, we're not as incompetent as it might appear. If I didn't feel strongly about the integrity of the company, I wouldn't be asking you to renew the contract."

"So the whole urgency to make all the repairs around the chateau and the list of repairmen you mentioned…"

"Just doing my job and trying to make sure we can at least collect the Nosenbergers' payment. It's not nearly enough, but it will help to keep the IRS off our backs."

"And your interest in the family's art collection?"

"Is just what I said—my attempt to help you retain the bulk of the estate. Not that I don't also want you to keep renting out the chateau."

Edmond wet his lips. "And as far as the Botticelli goes?" He paused a beat. "Tell me, in all honesty."

Shelley frowned. "The truth? Frankly—and please don't be offended, because I know how much your family prizes the drawing—but to tell you the truth…"

"Yes?" He felt his heart thumping.

"…I'm not convinced it's all that good. I know it's a study for one of his most famous paintings and therefore of historical interest. But I just don't believe it's worth nearly as much as you might think."

The jackhammering built in his chest. "Are you saying it's a fake?"

Now she'd really offended him. "More likely from the school of Botticelli or one of his followers. But an art expert couldn't possibly make a definitive statement one way or the other without intensive study, not to mention testing."

When he didn't respond, she winced. "Please, Edmond, I didn't mean to offend you. I'm only giving you my opinion, for whatever it's worth."

Edmond gazed past her to the ancient plains below, so dry, so full of their own secrets. Despite all his cynical instincts, he wanted to believe her. But he found himself holding back because he wasn't quite sure. And because, as she had said earlier, he was used to protecting himself.

Shelley could feel him slipping away. *What the heck.* If she was doomed anyway, she might as well reveal what was probably the most important reason she'd made the trek. "There *is* one more thing," she said tentatively, placing a hand on his chest to get his attention.

The combined pressure was almost too much. "Yes?"

Shelley balled up her fingers. "You know how I told you that I was used to traveling around to shore up Lionel's deals?"

He angled his chin and willed himself to breathe.

"Well, that wasn't true." She wet her lips. "I mean,

yeah, I make things happen for Dream Villas, but strictly as an office flunky. You see, I'm a regular whiz with the paperwork and making sure the properties are in order—but that's strictly from a distance, over the phone or via fax and e-mail. When it comes to face-to-face interactions, Lionel handles those. Let's just say that kind of activity is traditionally not my strength." She looked down. "But I really want it to be."

She squared her shoulders and stood up a little straighter, the top of her head level with his cheekbones. "I know it probably sounds ridiculous to someone like you, but the real reason I decided—no, I insisted—on coming here was to prove that I could venture out of my airless office, that I could abandon my boring life of picking up dry cleaning for my ex-boyfriend and having my best friend lecture me on which fork to use and not complaining when the coffee guy gives me the wrong change in the morning. Because I want to confront the world head-on, even if it means risking failure."

She was out of breath. Well, no one ever said confronting the world head-on was easy.

She waited.

And finally, after what seemed an eternity, he took her clenched hand in his. "I don't think it sounds ridiculous."

Shelley was too stunned to be relieved. "You don't?"

"No." He shook his head, and for the first time in the conversation, Edmond smiled. A real smile that crinkled the corners of his eyes. "I think it sounds… completely honest. And just like you, just like the

Shelley that I find so wonderful." He squeezed her hand. "Shelley, call Lionel."

"What? Now?" She was still digesting the news that Edmond found her wonderful. "I'm not sure he's there."

"Then leave a message. Tell him I want to renew the contract. I'll find a way—we'll find a way together—to retain the chateau. And tell him to come in person for the signing."

"You mean it?"

"Every word." His lips were almost but not quite within kissing distance.

"I'm so glad." And the next thing she knew, there wasn't any more distance. His lips made contact with hers, his mouth opened and his warmth invaded her in an aching sweetness.

And when the kiss was finished, Edmond slowly drew his head back. He felt euphoric. And horny as hell. To think that in the midst of a family disaster he had actually found someone genuine.

Someone he hoped would forgive him for using her to help catch her employer. Because if Shelley wasn't the one who'd stolen the Botticelli, it had to be Toynbee. After all, from the information Vincent had uncovered, Edmond already knew about the other art substitutions at properties on Dream Villas' roster.

But he couldn't risk telling her what he was now only starting to grasp—that somehow Lionel had wanted her here to divert the family's attention. He couldn't risk having her give away the whole thing when she made the call because he needed her to get Lionel here if he was going to nail him.

Edmond circled her in his arms, wanting to guard her vulnerability. Wanting to do more than that.

Don't be a selfish jerk, he rebuked himself silently. *You might not flinch at using her to nab Toynbee, but that doesn't mean you shouldn't wait until this whole mess is resolved.* Once that happened, he was prepared to be completely honest with her.

He rested his chin on the top of her head and gently brushed her hair away from the side of her face. The wind blew it back, so he twirled it around his finger and snagged it behind her ear. And with all the nobility that one would expect from someone who had learned to fence with a sword once owned by Louis XIV, the Sun King himself, he asked, "Do you want supper? The Oustau de Baumanière really is the jewel of all restaurants in the region."

Shelley leaned into his chest, savoring his strength, then peered up. She had always pictured a handsome man staring at her this way—adoringly, slightly nervous, with a band of light highlighting his smoldering features. It topped watching the end of *The Count of Monte Cristo* for the fourteenth time on video any day.

"I'm not hungry," she said. And she wasn't.

"Are you sure? They are famous for their truffle ravioli and *caladons*—a local specialty, a cake made with sweetened almond paste. It's irresistible, I assure you."

Shelley couldn't help smiling. "It will mark the

soul forever," she said, paraphrasing the line from the brochure. The late *comtesse* might have been a creep of the first order, but she didn't lack for insight.

Shelley raised one hand and stroked the back of his head. "I think we should skip dessert and go straight to the entertainment."

Edmond didn't blink. He didn't breathe either. But when he finally did, he managed to blurt out, "Are you saying what I think you're saying?"

"I'm saying that I think we should find out if there's a room at the inn."

12

LIKE MOST FRENCH HOTEL rooms, this one had wallpaper that—to put it kindly—made a bold statement. It was also only slightly larger than a steamer trunk and had a queen-size bed covered with enough down-filled pillows and duvets to have left scores of barnyards featherless.

The bed dominated the limited floor space. There were times when the French simply did not go for subtlety.

Shelley took a few steps through the door, and Edmond shut and locked it. Then he slowly turned to her, his hand reflexively reaching in his pocket for his lighter.

She let her bag slide to the floor, and without taking her eyes off Edmond, kicked it to the side.

His hand left his pocket.

With their eyes never leaving each other, they yanked off their shoes and tore off their clothes—nothing like cotton knit and a lack of buttons to speed up the process. And they threw themselves into each other's arms.

And there was nothing like naked bodies. Hot naked bodies.

Edmond kissed her mouth, her jaw, her neck. Shelley ran her fingers through his hair and scraped her lower teeth along the stubble on his cheek. Then he lifted her off the ground, and his mouth found her breast.

In the best of all possible worlds, Edmond would have liked to think that when it came to sexual gymnastics, he was as agile as the next superhero. But for some reason—maybe to do with the blood pounding at his temples, or maybe to do with the fact that Shelley's body, while not particularly heavy was not of the featherweight category—he found his arms slowly start to give way.

Oh hell, maybe he wasn't a superhero after all.

So he staggered forward, refusing to let go and praying he was headed in the general vicinity of the bed.

They banged clumsily into a massive armoire.

Shelley pulled her lips from his. She gasped. "Watch out for the furniture."

Edmond glanced over her shoulder. "Don't worry. It's a reproduction." He kissed her hard and fast and maneuvered valiantly to the left.

The back of his knees ran into the bed frame, and he sank down, sitting up on the cloudy softness of the duvet and carrying Shelley with him. She landed on top, poised above his erection.

She placed her hands on his shoulders and let her body sink down, her mouth dropping open as the intense, slick heat filled her. She raised back up and lowered herself once more with an agonizing slowness.

Edmond groaned. He grabbed her hips, and together they fell backward on the bed. Shelley arched her head back, her hair brushing her shoulders, and shut her eyes. All she could think of—and she wasn't sure if she would call it *thinking*—was that those suggestive phrases and dirty words that sometimes accompanied heated lovemaking sounded better in French.

And the amazing way a finger placed just so and the heel of a palm rubbed in a certain way…oh, and if lips were applied with just the right pressure…that the total combination could produce a welling of desire that left a woman gasping, "Stop" and begging, "More."

Well, those fingers and palms and lips all seemed to function so much better when they came attached to Edmond. And it wasn't just the artful mechanics of it—of that Shelley was convinced. Though far be it from her, a trained art historian, to deny his artistry.

No, it was something more. Something that went beyond sensory responses and sexual chemistry, something that produced more combustion energy than any scientific lab.

And wouldn't you know, when he'd loosened his tight grip on her buttocks (no doubt she'd have marks in the morning), and after she'd just climaxed in a way that catapulted flashing stars to the back of her eyelids and produced a concussive impact on whatever gray matter was left in her brain—after all that had happened and he'd thrust one last time, a giant shudder wracking his body as he finally allowed himself to climax—he'd said, upon barely managing to recover but still joined deep within her, *"Je suis complet."* I am complete.

That sounded great in any language.

SHELLEY LAY CURLED UP IN BED next to Edmond. They'd managed to crawl under the duvet and were cuddling each other in a mixture of exhaustion and disbelief. On the floor lay the remnants of Isabelle's picnic hamper—a tin of pâté de foie gras, a crisp baguette and a bottle of Sauternes. Shelley had only finished brushing the last of the baguette crumbs off the sheet. "Do we need to contact your aunts?" she asked.

He kissed her forehead. "Relax."

That wasn't hard. Her eyelids were sinking to half-mast. "But won't they wonder where we are?"

"I think they can guess." He snuggled closer and rubbed the underside of her breast with his thumb. "Besides—" he kissed her ear "—I think they will be secretly delighted that we're not coming home tonight."

Shelley nuzzled the side of her head against his cheek. "I don't think it will be such a big secret."

"Shelley?"

"Yes?" She loved the way he said her name.

"Before you fall asleep, would you mind calling Lionel? In the midst of everything else, we forgot to do it. And now that I've made up my mind, I'd like to move with signing the contracts as soon as possible. Unless you are too tired?"

"No, of course not. Anyway, it's wonderful news to share. And Lionel's coming will allow me to gloat in my triumph." She twisted her neck around and grinned with enormous self-satisfaction.

Edmond kissed her on the forehead. "And you deserve every bit of it. In fact, why don't you tell him I won't agree to the deal unless he shows up? That way I can praise you to the heavens the whole time he's here." He hated lying to her. But he did it anyway. "I'll get your phone. It's in your bag, no?"

She nodded and watched him pad naked across the room. There were times when life was just too good to be true.

He grabbed her purse and slipped back under the covers. An engraved medallion hanging from a short silver chain around his neck rapped against his chest.

"What's that anyway?" she asked, sitting up.

Edmond looked down. "The medallion? It's the symbol of the Montforts—a porcupine."

"Figures." She pulled out her phone. "Family is ever close to your heart." She punched in the office number and waited. Again, no one picked up, and the answering machine kicked in.

"He's not there?" Edmond propped himself up on an elbow.

Shelley held up her hand for quiet. She left a message on the machine, letting Lionel know the good news and the fact that Edmond requested his presence at the signing. "Maybe he's out wining and dining some new property owner?" she said offhandedly as she went back to the phone's menu.

"All day?"

"You have to take 'wining and dining' in the most liberal of senses when it comes to Lionel." She scrolled down to the in-box, just to make sure she hadn't missed any calls from Lionel. No, but there were two messages in her mailbox—one from Abigail, the other from Paul.

She glanced up and saw Edmond eyeing her intently. The duvet had fallen away from her torso, and her breasts were in plain sight—and *not* sagging, she was pleased to say. And apparently, from the way Edmond's eyes had turned suddenly black, he was also pleased. Mightily pleased.

What to do? Listen to well-meaning lectures on how to use grape shears and the dangers of degenerate foreign types? Or have yet another bout of no-holes-barred—she meant that metaphorically, of course, or did she?—sex?

Gosh, the choices!

Shelley angled her head just so, so she could get a prime view of one of the nicest chests to be found in this or any other province of France. Seeing her interest, Edmond raised his eyebrows and grinned. And, if she were not mistaken, blushed.

She turned off her phone, dumped it in her bag and shoved the whole thing to the floor. "Edmond?" she asked sweetly.

He cocked his head. "Can I get you something else?"

She sidled closer. "Honestly?"

He cupped her chin in his hand. "Honestly, *chérie*."

"Well, in that case, I can think of several things."

And so could he.

THE NEXT MORNING, EDMOND waited until he heard Shelley turn on the shower. Then he slipped his cell phone out of his trouser pocket. He hit the second number on speed dial. The first was his aunts'.

"Any further word on Toynbee?" he asked without preamble. "He hasn't been answering at the office in Philadelphia, and I have a suspicion he may be en route."

Vincent didn't bother with the formalities either. "You're right, as usual. The FBI reported that he took a flight to Amsterdam. Unfortunately, the Dutch authorities lost him after he boarded the train from Schiphol Airport into the city."

Edmond swore, not using any of the highfalutin oaths that appeared in left-wing journals. No, he spat out the kind uttered in the back streets of Marseilles and usually accompanied by a knife—a very sharp knife. "How hard can it be to keep track of an aging crook who dresses like Errol Flynn and wears pink ascots? Don't they realize how important he is? We are talking about a major art thief."

Vincent grunted in agreement. "You think he'll show up at the chateau?"

"It's only a question of when." Especially if Toynbee received Shelley's last message.

"What about the woman?" Vincent asked. "She is still in Aix, correct?"

"Yes, I've been keeping close tabs on her—very close." Edmond glanced at the bathroom door and thought of Shelley—wonderful, sexy Shelley—standing with her eyes shut as the soap bubbles and streams of water sluiced down her body.

"You haven't found that awkward?"

Edmond cleared his throat. "Not at all." He ignored the rising pressure in his pants. "In fact, the task has been relatively simple since she moved into the chateau at my aunts' insistence."

"Tant mieux." So much the better. Vincent punctuated his remark with a snort. "Maybe you'll catch her with her hands in the cookie jar, eh?"

Edmond thought of where her hands—and his— had already been. He shook his head and put his mind back to business. "Actually the longer I'm with *Mademoiselle* McCleery, the more I think that we were too hasty in our assumptions. I'm starting to believe that we should look elsewhere."

"You really think so?"

Something in Vincent's voice had Edmond on alert. "You've found something to the contrary?"

"The list of local repairmen you gave me yesterday? The one she compiled?"

"Yes?" He ran his hand through his hair.

"It looks like we may have hit pay dirt."

The shower turned off. And so did Edmond's sense of euphoria. Once more it seemed happiness was a greatly overrated feeling. He should have stuck to his instincts.

"IF YOU COULD CUT THE ENGINE and just coast up the rest of the drive, that would be great," Shelley asked as they entered the gates to the chateau. The drive back from Les Baux had been surprisingly quiet, but she assumed that Edmond was just tired from lack of sleep.

"Why? Are you concerned that my aunts will see you in the same clothes as yesterday? They are probably well aware that you didn't come back." Nevertheless, he did as she asked and cut the engine. He was still mulling over the information that Vincent had sprung on him at the end of the conversation.

"I know it doesn't make any sense, but there you go." She skipped up the front steps. Despite minimal rest, she felt surprisingly energized, giddy even. If she weren't careful, she'd start emitting that Sandra Dee glow. The thought should have horrified her.

Shelley didn't care.

"Allow me." Edmond held open the door and followed her into the foyer. The banquet-size Shiraz carpet, a gift to the family from the Ottoman ambassador—back in the days when there *was* an Ottoman Empire—muffled their steps. It did nothing to soften his disappointment.

"I'll just be a minute," she said, heading for the majestic double staircase. She paused halfway up and glanced back. "You know—" she pointed around the room "—I still can't believe I'm staying in a place like this. Let me tell you, this is a long way from Schenectady."

Edmond waited with one foot on the bottom stair. And was struck by an eerie sense of déjà vu. The way he was standing now—with Shelley on the stairs above him—was almost an exact replica of how his father had posed before entering the ballroom for the annual formal party to celebrate his mother's birthday, which conveniently coincided with the first grape pressing.

Standing ramrod straight, his father would watch while his mother made a grand entrance down the staircase in her latest Givenchy gown. The Montfort tiara—another victim of his stepgrandmother's greed—would gleam in her rich mahogany hair, and laughing voices would fill the air.

He regarded Shelley. She had one arm sturdily holding the shoulder strap of her purse. The other remained extended outward. With her riotous red hair and natural grace, and even her casual clothes and sneakers, she seemed to fit into the surroundings—old-fashioned but relaxed, gracious yet unafraid to show backbone, full of color and life but able to wield a hammer with enviable dexterity. How ironic that the one person who seemed to be involved with stealing from the family actually looked as if she belonged here.

"Do you hear voices?" Shelley's question interrupted his daydreaming. She turned to the front parlor. "I'm sure I heard voices. And not just your aunts'. If I didn't know better…" Her voice trailed off as she descended quickly and crossed the hallway.

Edmond caught up with her footsteps. She was right. It wasn't a memory that he had conjured up. There *were* voices. Several voices. Voices speaking English.

Immediately the adrenaline started to surge. He forced himself to walk slowly.

The wooden doors to the salon were closed. Shelley put her ear close to the paneling. No, she wasn't completely crazy. She turned back to Edmond. His expression was deadly serious. "Should we knock?" she asked in a whisper.

"Don't be ridiculous. This is my house. I don't care if it's the mayor of Philadelphia himself," he replied, sounding very countlike. In one decisive movement, he turned the handle and swept open the door.

Talk about a conversation stopper.

13

THERE WAS DEAD SILENCE AND several pairs of nervously blinking eyes.

About the only person from Philadelphia not in the room *was* the mayor.

Oh, and Lionel.

"Abigail?" Shelley asked in disbelief. Then she pivoted on her left foot. "Paul?" she announced with greater shock.

"You see, we said it was only a matter of time before they returned from their little sojourn," Marie-Jeanne announced, dropping her pearls with a hollow thump to her chest. She wore a braided tweed Chanel jacket that any vintage shop worth, well, its Worth gowns, could sell in less than a heartbeat.

"Shell-ee, Edmond, you must be famished. Have some scones." Isabelle did her best to smooth over the awkwardness of the situation by, as usual, plying food.

Abigail rested her teacup on the low table in front of the Napoleon III couch she was sitting on. She uncrossed her long legs and rose with seamless elegance. She was the only person on God's green earth who could wear linen trousers *and* not wrinkle them. "Didn't you get my phone message?"

"And mine?" Paul stood abruptly. His teacup clattered out of his large hand.

Shelley stared for another beat. No, two. "Yes. No. I mean, yes, I got them but no, I didn't have a chance to listen to them." She smiled a tight-lipped but gracious smile. "And no, thank you, Isabelle. It looks wonderful, but I'm not hungry."

There was a loud clearing of a throat from off to the side.

"Oh, yes, how could I have forgotten? Abigail Braithwaite, Paul Gufstavsen, this is Edmond, the count de Montfort."

"*Mademoiselle.*" Edmond kissed Abigail's hand, which had her drooling.

And which had Shelley wondering why Edmond had never kissed *her* hand, even though admittedly he had kissed quite a few other places.

Then he exchanged what looked like a bone-crushing handshake with Paul. "*Monsieur* Gufstavsen."

"That's *Dr.* Paul Gufstavsen," Paul amended. He tried to be manly and not wince when Edmond tightened the grip a few more notches.

Shelley ignored the whole exchange. She couldn't deal with ridiculous male-bonding rituals when she had more distressing questions on her mind. Did they *so* not trust her? "But how? Why?" she asked incredulously.

"We flew Continental to Paris and then took the

TGV to Marseilles," Abigail recited their itinerary. "I explained to Paul that everyone in Europe takes the train—it's so civilized. From there, it was just a question of a taxi."

Was Abigail rambling? It wasn't like her to ramble.

"I think what Shelley means," Paul interrupted, "is what brings us here so suddenly?"

Abigail pursed her lips. "Yes, sorry, my mistake."

And with that lack of catty riposte, Shelley knew that either she had entered the twilight zone or her friend had had a full-frontal lobotomy.

Abigail stepped forward. "I think you should listen to the messages."

"Perhaps you could just tell me?" Shelley offered.

Paul lowered his voice an octave. "It's private."

"Shelley." Edmond placed his hand on her elbow.

She caught Paul frowning and realized Edmond's gesture was not entirely meant for her.

"Why don't you excuse yourself briefly to listen to your messages?" Edmond suggested. "While you're doing that, we'll have some tea, and Dr. Gufstavsen can explain to us why the American medical profession is in such crisis."

Nobody moved. Except for Boris the cat, who took that moment to enter through an open French door. All heads watched as the feline slalomed lazily among the carved legs of the chairs.

"Please, be seated," Edmond urged with an air of supreme authority. He'd obviously read more than his fair share of biographies of the Bourbon kings.

Abigail and Paul sat instantly. Marie-Jeanne went

back to patting her pearls. Isabelle reached for another cup and saucer.

And Edmond sat, looking pleased with the results. He shooed away the cat, who was taking a decided interest in the clotted cream. "*Tante* Isabelle, the scones look marvelous. If you please…"

Lobotomies. The whole lot of them, Shelley thought, and she turned and left them to babble among themselves.

SHE TOOK THE CALLS OUTSIDE, seeking comfort—and perhaps enlightenment—in the sunshine.

The first was Abigail's:

"Shelley, call me ASAP. That's 'as soon as possible', in case you aren't up on the business lingo."

Shelley held the phone away from her ear. "Strange as it may seem, I learned that phrase sometime after mastering the use of a soupspoon." She deleted the call and waited for Paul's message:

"Shelley, it's Paul. I know you think I'm always being critical—"

Shelley turned her eyes up to the cloudless sky.

"—but you really should keep this turned on if you expect to have people get through to you. Anyway, I've just come off another double shift—Maureen, one of the other residents, went on maternity leave. Sometimes I wonder about women and if they're truly committed to their profession."

Shelley was just about to delete the message, when Paul's next words stopped her.

"Abigail is here with me, very distraught, not knowing who to turn to."

"To whom to turn," Shelley corrected but continued to listen.

"She told me about the FBI stopping by her office and asking what she knew about Dream Villas and Lionel and you."

Shelley could feel her throat constrict. "Don't you mean the IRS?" she asked in a tiny voice.

"Anyhow, these government agents started asking Abigail about the company's finances… Sorry, Abigail says I shouldn't talk about it over the phone. Something about the possibility of a tap on the line."

The tightness was traveling up her jaw, pressing on her ears. Shelley wasn't sure she could still hear. But she could, just enough.

"I had a bad feeling about this trip right from the start, and this just confirms it. Oh, and despite what you said before leaving, I found it perfectly straightforward to pick up the dry cleaning. But I'm surprised you never told me I could get my shirts boxed and not on a hanger. Abigail told me that's how her father's always had his done."

Shelley switched off the phone, too stunned to be amazed.

SHE REENTERED THE FOYER AND looked around. Abigail and Paul were coming toward her from the salon. "Are the Montforts still in there?" She motioned with her head.

"Not anymore," Abigail answered. "While you were out of the room, some workman—"

"Marius?"

"Yes, that's it, Marius. Anyway, he came running in, and I couldn't quite understand, but he seemed to be going on and on about some emergency upstairs. Then Edmond and his aunts excused themselves to go check on it with him, but as they were leaving, the count received a call on his cell. Some kind of emergency—something to do with toothpaste—that couldn't be put off."

Paul leaned forward and put his hand to the side of his mouth. "The whole family's a bit strange, if you ask me. Too much inbreeding. Did you see how all of them had exactly the same pronounced bridge to their noses?" he whispered loudly.

Shelley put her fingers to her forehead. She wasn't sure what was worse—Paul's stage mannerisms or the messages on her phone. No, she knew which. "Forget the Montforts and their noses, would you? I'm still reeling from the fact that you decided to track me down. And what's all this about the FBI?"

Abigail placed the back of her hand to her brow.

In Shelley's opinion, she, Paul and Toto, the Miele repairman—the whole lot of them—should get together and form a Gilbert and Sullivan troupe.

"As if I would abandon you in your moment of need?" Abigail implored. "As for those FBI agents—they had me so worried. What do you think Lionel's done? Slept with someone he shouldn't?"

"That's not a federal crime, last I heard," Shelley

said in a world-weary tone. It was remarkable how a couple of days spent in "old Europe" made her view life with a jaundiced eye.

"Unless it was with J. Edgar Hoover," Paul said.

"Paul, J. Edgar Hoover is dead," Shelley reminded him.

"So? Stranger things have happened."

Abigail and Shelley were silent.

"Eeew," Shelley finally said. "Anyway, it's not about Lionel's sex life. It's about nonpayment of back taxes."

"Shelley." Abigail stepped forward, an impressive figure, even if she did have a fanny pack strapped to her waist. "Federal agents do not come to the offices of a suspect's acquaintances unless the back taxes involved are related to other nefarious activities."

Only Abigail would say "nefarious" in a sentence. Never mind. "You mean things like the Mob?"

Abigail nodded and Paul joined in a beat later. They looked like bad synchronized swimmers.

"Oh," Shelley said.

"Oh, is right. And I think you should come home," Abigail said.

"On the next possible flight. We can all go together and take your rental car so that Count Edmond doesn't have to drive us," Paul said. "For all you know, he could be in on the hanky-panky."

"Hanky-panky!" Shelley slanted him a vulturelike look. Though with all Edmond's bizarre dental-product emergencies, Paul might actually have a point.

"Look, Shelley, with Lionel missing, I hate to be the bearer of bad news, but you don't even know if you have a job, let alone if Dream Villas is still in existence," Abigail informed her.

"I agree." Paul nodded earnestly. "And in cases like this I think you should listen to Abigail's more experienced judgment." He frowned, then shifted his gaze and smiled affectionately at Abigail.

She patted his shoulder. "I'm glad someone listens."

Shelley moved her head back and forth. Things had progressed at a rapid and unsuspected pace since last she'd seen them over cheesesteaks.

Abigail broke from her reverie, finally aware that someone else was in the room. She furrowed her brow in an awkward sympathy, quite like the one she assumed when telling clients they'd been slapped with a palimony suit. "I hope you're not upset— about Paul and myself."

"Of course I'm not upset," Shelley replied. And the truth of the matter was, she wasn't. Not in the tiniest bit. "Just a little surprised, that's all."

"I guess it developed as a result of your little adventure—" Abigail started to explain.

"Abigail, I am not on a 'little adventure,' as you put it. This is not some Pee-Wee Herman movie." The new Shelley was no longer a doormat.

"We know, we know," Paul broke in. Shelley doubted that he knew at all. "It's just that under the circumstances, Abigail and I, we sort of bonded."

Shelley had a gluelike image forming in her head.

"You know the old saying about opposites attracting?" Abigail asked. "Well, that's precisely what happened to us—one of those magnetic force things.

Besides, Paul appreciates the fact that I'm a strong woman. He likes that I have a take-charge personality."

"*Mademoiselle* Sheell-eey." A baleful cry erupted from the top of the stairway.

Shelley turned to see Marius descending toward her and she wondered if she had any Advil in her bag. She set her jaw. "*Oui, Marius, nous avons un problème?*" *Yes, Marius, we have a problem?*

"*C'est le 'ot toob.'*"

Marius' Provençal accent was particularly strong under duress—as in now—and Shelley wasn't quite sure what he meant. "*Comment?*" *What?* she asked politely.

"*Le 'ot toob.'*"

Shelley still didn't get it.

Finally Marius made a spitting noise with his mouth and mimicked water rising all around him.

"Oh, *the hot tub.*" The light dawned. "Something's wrong with the hot tub? Is that where Marie-Jeanne and Isabelle are now?"

Marius nodded gravely.

In the scheme of things, this was something she could handle.

Abigail held up her hand and twiddled her fingers. "I'm afraid it's my fault. I thought it would be lovely to have a bath after the long journey, even though Paul warned me that I'd probably use all the hot water, this being Europe and all."

"Nonsense. I had a five-hundred gallon hot-water heater installed three years ago," Shelley replied, taking his comment personally.

"Anyway, there was plenty of hot water, but I'm afraid now the bath won't drain."

"It won't drain?" Shelley mentally began going through her list of repairmen for the name of the plumber. "Then I had better call the plumber."

"No need." Edmond strode in from the kitchen. "I already called him when I heard about the problem."

Shelley was dumbfounded. "You called the plumber? How did you even know who the plumber was?"

"From the list of repairmen." He winced. An unfortunate slip of the tongue.

"That's right. I saw that the aunts keep a copy in the kitchen." Then she noticed his awkward expression. "Sorry if it was beneath you."

"Nothing I couldn't handle." Another bullet dodged. There was only so much luck to go around. And he didn't even believe in luck.

"Anyhow, I thought you were tied up with some life-or-death struggle at work?" Shelley asked.

"I'm hoping it doesn't come to that." It was the truth.

Marie-Jeanne and Isabelle appeared at the top of the staircase.

"Everything is under control, no?" Marie-Jeanne inquired.

"As well as it *can* be under the circumstances. Not to worry," Edmond reassured her. He had his own more pressing concerns.

"I told Marius there was no need to take you from your friends, Shell-ee," Isabelle said by way of apology.

"Nonsense. Who better to deal with an emergency

than I?" Shelley replied. And to remember the nominative case.

And then Edmond's cell phone rang. Yet again.

He growled and answered it.

Abigail backed up. Paul backed up.

Marie-Jeanne reached for her pearls. Isabelle fingered her moonstone ring.

Edmond clipped his phone shut.

"What is it this time? A run on dental floss?" Shelley asked.

Edmond narrowed his eyes. "I won't even bother to explain." And he didn't, instead turning and leaving abruptly.

Shelley raised her eyebrows to their limit and ever so slowly and deliberately turned her gaze toward everybody else who stood by—everybody but Marius, who was tiptoeing away as quickly as possible.

"What now?" Paul asked.

What indeed?

It took Shelley all of a second to decide. Oh, all right, two and a half seconds. At which point she told herself that if at the age of fifteen she could drive her sister Emily to the emergency ward while stemming the blood flowing profusely from her forehead—Emily had mistakenly thought she was capable of vaulting off the family picnic table—she could certainly deal with this.

"Marius, *arrêtez-vous.*" *Marius, stop,* she called out. "After you and I check upstairs, we are going to look at the peeling plaster in the gallery."

"You're going to look at the peeling plaster in the

gallery?" Paul stammered. From his tone you would have thought she had suggested the dissolution of the Lutheran synod.

"But what about—" Abigail made wavy hand motions "—you know?"

Shelley thought that Abigail should really *not* consider becoming a mime as an alternative career. Still, she got the message. "Regarding the matter that brought you here, the earliest flights home are scheduled for midday tomorrow. That being the case, there's absolutely no point sitting around and being nervous, not when there's something useful to be done. And as for something for you two to do? I know. Why don't you take my rental car—" she fished the keys out of her bag "—and drive to Aix? There's any number of cafés on the Cours Mirabeau. I'm sure you'll enjoy them, as well as the many boutiques offering tasteful designer items that are marginally less expensive on this side of the Atlantic." She held up the keys, waiting to see who would take them.

Abigail hesitated only a moment. "Let me. I know how to drive stick shift." She patted her fanny pack and, indirectly, the Visa cards inside. Paul trailed behind as they headed out the door.

Shelley looked to the aunts. They looked back with their customary mixture of politeness and cluelessness. "I'm so sorry for the intrusion of my friends from Philadelphia," she said.

"It is not a problem." Marie-Jeanne dismissed her apologies. "Once, the Earl of Faversham arrived with his six corgis, all unannounced."

"And he insisted on having coddled eggs—for the dogs," Isabelle said by way of assurance. She hesitated. "Your friends will not want coddled eggs, will they?"

"I don't expect so," Shelley said.

"Then everything will be fine." Isabelle beamed. *If only.*

14

Marius may have been willing, but that didn't mean he was competent. Shelley had to help him find a utility cord and a stepladder so that they could erect some extra lighting in the gallery and get a better look at the damaged plaster.

She finished tying back the last of the heavy green velvet curtains and turned to face the problem area in the corner. For once, the art collection was illuminated enough to appreciate its fine quality, especially the small ivory. The delicacy of its intricate carving and the fanciful expressions on the faces of the animals were clearly visible. Shelley had to restrain herself from running her finger along the surface.

And the painting by Duccio of St. George also took on a renewed vigor. The accumulation of dirt on the oil's surface couldn't hide the meandering gold lines edging the saint's cloak and the dragon's extended wings. Shelley peered closely. The dragon, the symbol of sin, had blue eyes. *Hmm*. Wonder who that reminded her of?

Shelley straightened up and walked to the other end of the room, passing the Botticelli with far less interest than she paid the blistering and flaking plaster down the side of the wall.

And she would have gone on completely ignoring it if Marius hadn't cleared his throat. She stopped and glanced over her shoulder. The workman raised a finger. Even though it was permanently bent—an incident involving *boules* and a rival team from Nîmes—she saw that he was pointing toward the bottom of the large drawing. "*Sheell.*" He pointed more emphatically. "*Sheell.*"

Shelley wasn't sure if he was having some kind of seizure.

His eyes fluttered and he pointed haltingly again. She mentally reviewed the ABC's of artificial respiration.

"*Sheell,*" he repeated. "*Comme vous vous appelez. Sheell-Sheell-eey.*"

"Huh?" She had her mouth open. And then it hit her what he was saying. *Shell, like your name—shell, Shelley.*

Great. On top of everything else, Marius was choosing today of all day's to make tentative overtures. She smiled tightly, aware that this was a delicate situation. Particularly if she wanted to get the wall fixed. "That's right, shell, Shelley." She nodded toward the drawing—

Then stopped with her neck in midbounce.

She took a step closer. "*Pardonez-moi.*" She indicated his hand, and he pulled it back.

She leaned forward and examined the drawing— the scallop shell, Venus's feet, her legs, her hand demurely half covering her breasts, her coy smile and wavy hair....

Shelley bolted upright and blurted out a four-letter word that even Marius, with his limited English, understood. A goat herder in Uzbekistan would understand it—after all, it was something he came across on a daily basis.

Then she uttered another with equal force that had Marius gasping. And she wasn't taking the Lord's name in vain.

It was another lord's name. Edmond.

Now she knew why he had been dogging her repeatedly about the Botticelli. His question about whether she thought it was a fake came back to haunt her. Could it really mean what she thought it did? "Him and his toothpaste wars!" She was so upset, she actually used an objective pronoun as a subject.

From outside came the sound of a car rolling up the stone drive. Shelley walked to the door, ready to confront the count. If only she had a sword, a rapier. She didn't have the faintest idea how to fence, but she was pretty sure that if she thrust it at point-blank range, she was bound to damage at least one vital organ. Preferably his heart.

She grabbed the massive handle and heaved the door open.

Only it wasn't Edmond. *"C'est le plombier." It's the plumber,* she told Marius. "And he's parking around the back. I'll just go to meet him."

"I'll come with you," Marius said nobly, even though it was plain to see his heart wasn't in it.

She strode determinedly to the back of the house. "No!" she ordered, freezing him in his slow-moving tracks. "You stay and watch the 'sheell.'"

"*MONSIEUR!* HELLO! YOO-HOO!" Shelley waved wildly to get the plumber's attention. *Yoo-hoo?* That was so like her mother. This is what this whole episode was doing—it was turning her into her mother.

Shelley skipped down the back stairs and began marching at top speed. The plumber was dressed in the ubiquitous blue jumpsuit of French workmen and wore a bandanna around his neck. From a distance, it looked as if it were held in place by a metal ring. He carried a large oblong box and was walking away from the chateau. More precisely, he was practically running—rather gracefully, mind you, but definitely in the wrong direction. More specifically, toward the garden wall.

"*Monsieur,*" Shelley called out again, but he had already ducked through the opening.

She glimpsed around. Now when she could have used the whole entourage, there was nobody to be found. She was about to head back to the chateau when she saw Boris the cat perched on the rim of a large garden urn. Its paws were placed tightly together amidst a spray of blue lobelia. It arched its neck and raised its face. The metal fastener on its collar glittered in the sun.

And then she remembered. The Montfort porcupine medallion around Edmond's neck. The way he had insisted they visit the cave. The way he had suggested that there was something more to see farther inside.

She didn't waver.

IT WAS DARK—DARK ENOUGH that Shelley could hardly see where she was going. But she kept her hand in contact with the damp walls to help guide her as she followed the bobbing flashlight ahead. She had only been in the cave a day ago, so her short-term memory should provide some additional guidance.

Down the long tunnel to the open cavern with Old Faithful. Next Snow White and the Seven Dwarfs. Only it no longer seemed so amusing, especially when she realized how she'd been the one to jump to the conclusion that Edmond was interested in opening the site to tourists. She was surprised he hadn't laughed at the time. Though come to think of it, he had made fun of the idea of having gaudy colored lights and tacky names for the rock shapes.

She shifted her eyes back and forth, trying to decide which way to go. To the right, yes, to the right. Past the handprint on the wall. She thought of her own hand touching the same stones as the prehistoric dwellers.

Then she saw the light flashing to her left.

She stepped cautiously. Was this where they'd stopped to look at the cave paintings of the horses? The sound of rushing water grew louder.

The light in front of her continued to move on, ducking down and around. Shelley sped up. She couldn't lose sight of it now that she was entering uncharted territory. She felt the wall, found the low opening and stooped down.

The floor of the cave dropped without warning. She slipped, stumbling to her knees. And landed in an inch of freezing-cold water. It covered her hands and soaked her pant legs. She must have landed smack-dab in an underground stream.

The light turned and exposed her.

She gasped. "Lionel!"

"You sound as if you were expecting someone else."

Shelley scrambled to her feet. "I was. I caught a glimpse of something metal around your neck and it made me think of someone else." She peered closely. "But I can see that I was wrong—it's just a stickpin in your ascot."

"Not *just* a stickpin—it's *the* diamond-and-platinum stickpin that Queen Victoria gave to Prince Albert on their twentieth wedding anniversary. It's considered very lucky." Lionel was gravely offended.

"I'm glad—for the queen, for Albert and for you." She couldn't have cared less. "But even more to the point, why are you wearing those clothes?" She dried her hands on the seat of her pants and waited for an explanation.

"It see-eemed the appropriate form of attire."

"For a plumber maybe—" She stopped. "Lionel, what's going on here?"

"I've come for the Botticelli."

"The Botticelli? If you mean the one in the gallery, I hate to tell you—it's a fake."

"I know, I exchanged it for the ree-eal one."

"The real one?"

"Yes, the real one." He placed the long metal box he'd been carrying on the ground and reached behind a massive stalagmite. He held up a plastic mailing tube. "I've been hiding it here until I could retrieve it." Then he bent down and unhooked the latch to the box, slipping the tube inside. "And now I've got it."

From off in the darkness, a lighter flicked on. "I wouldn't be so sure."

Shelley spied the outlines of a gun.

In Edmond's right hand.

Omigod! Her suspicions had been right. Edmond knew the Botticelli in the gallery was a fake, had somehow found the drawing here and was going to sell it for himself.

No wonder he'd initially balked at the idea of selling off the collection. He was afraid the appraisers would discover the Botticelli wasn't genuine. Of course, the real drawing was his to do with as he wanted, but if he sold it, his aunts would find out and be acutely disappointed. For all his talk of preserving the family's heritage, he was really stealing part of it for himself.

Or maybe he wasn't being so selfish? Maybe he was planning to carry out some kind of insurance scam—keep the real one hidden and collect the money on the stolen work and then use the funds to pay off the taxes and retain the villa?

No matter what, he was wrong and it was illegal any way you looked at it.

Shelley thought of their exchange by the fountain, when she'd blabbed about how much she disliked her job and measly salary. He probably had figured he could convince her to go in with him and that's why he had insisted on taking her to the cave. He'd rather cut her in for part of the deal than risk having his plan—whichever one it was—backfire.

And to think he had been the one to stress the importance of honesty and open communication! Talk about being duped! She quickly replayed more of their conversations in her head and realized she'd been an even bigger fool than she'd first imagined. Not only had she refused to go far enough into the cave, she'd later admitted that she wouldn't bother auctioning off the Botticelli—inferior workmanship, she'd claimed at the time. He must have been laughing all the way.

"Kick the box this way, Toynbee," Edmond ordered.

Lionel feebly pushed the box with the sole of his boot. It scraped along the stones.

"Edmond," Shelley pleaded.

He slanted his head in her direction.

"Don't do this." Call her a sap, but even though she hated what he'd done, she still couldn't bring herself to hate *him*. Because she knew that deep down he was a lonely, sensitive man, a man who had given her an incredible night of passion—passion that had come from the heart. If he didn't deserve redemption, who did?

"Edmond," she repeated. "Don't do this. I'm sure we can work things out. Let me help."

Edmond scowled. "What? The same way you came to Aix to help him?"

"Who, Lionel? Of course I originally came to help him. You think I'd let Dream Villas go up in smoke?"

Edmond shook his head. "I should have trusted my instincts. But, no. All your talk about needing to prove your worth, the whole IRS story—I really fell for it." He jerked his gun to the side, then back at her. "Go stand next to him," he barked.

Shelley barely shuffled a couple of inches. She didn't want to get in too close contact with either of them.

"I must say, as con artists go, you are definitely one of the best I have ever run across," Edmond sneered. "I suppose you're going to tell me some other story as to why I find you here—with him and with the Botticelli? No wonder you didn't want to come farther. You knew what would be here!"

"Wait a minute!" Shelley protested. "I knew nothing of the Botticelli."

And then Shelley suddenly saw things with a clarity usually reserved for seers and insider traders. She eyed Lionel. "The Botticelli's not the only phony, is it? There is no problem with the IRS, there are no back taxes, no screwups with my paperwork, right?"

"I'm delighted to say that Uncle Sam is the lee-east of my worries. Thanks to your usual efficiency, our taxes have been squeaky clean."

"But if you didn't need the money to hold off the IRS, why send me here?"

Lionel shrugged. "Isn't it obvious? When that fax came about the lease, I knew I had to do something.

I couldn't have potential buyers or inspectors snoo-oooping around the place, discovering that the Botticelli in the gallery was a fake. I needed to buy some time to retrieve the real thing."

"You used me." Shelley was outraged. "Not only did you use me to buy time, you used my efforts to fix this place to help your disguise. All you had to do was wait for me to call a repairman, and there you'd be, in disguise as a plumber to collect the real Botticelli. So *you* were the one who originally blocked up the hot tub, not Abigail!"

"No, that bro-oke all on its own. Lucky for me. You see, I had had the idea to damage the washing machine and I had already bribed the local plumber to let me take his place. Then he tells me this mo-orning that an appliance repairman fixes washing machines, which was horrifying, to say the lea-east. Fortunately, when the call came through for the hot tub, I felt my prayers had be-en answered." He actually sounded pleased with his predicament.

"This is all very enlightening and will write up nicely in my report," Edmond interrupted. "But as much as I would love to stay here and chat, I really need you two to turn around and put your hands behind your backs."

Lionel did as he was told, but Shelley stood there, ignoring Edmond and instead digesting the full import of what Lionel had just said. "You didn't realize about the washing machine because you've never bothered to find out anything about how to manage these properties, have you?" Shelley's voice got quieter and quieter as her anger rose.

Edmond focused on Shelley. "That's enough. Turn around." His voice, by contrast, was increasingly louder and louder.

"Well, there re-ee-eally was no need, was there, my dee-ear? You always fixed everything so efficiently."

And that really got Shelley. She stalked over to Lionel, placing herself between Edmond and him. She pointed a finger right at his nose. "You slimeball. I hope those BOTOX injections leave you with permanent lumps and scarring. I hope you end up with all sorts of venereal diseases that cause your dick to shrivel up and fall off."

God, that felt good. For once, she'd actually said what she thought.

"Shelley, I'm not going to ask you again!" Edmond shouted. "Move to the side and put your hands behind your back."

"And what will you do if I don't?" Tearing her eyes away from Lionel, she slanted Edmond a furious glance. "From near as I can figure out, you knew about the real Botticelli being here the whole time, or part of it. Whatever." She shook her head. "Lionel may have been the one to make the switch, but in your own way, you're just as guilty. As if *I* should feel the need to defend my innocence to *you*?"

She saw Edmond's eyes dart from hers to Lionel's.

"Shelley," he said slowly.

She rotated her neck and saw that Lionel was holding a gun to her temple.

"Thank you-uu for the diversion, She-el-ley, dear." He nodded toward Edmond. "You wouldn't want me to hurt the lady, would you Mo-ontfort? Tarnish your aristocratic sensibility of fair play?"

"You forget. I'm one of the black sheep of the family. I missed out on the fair-play gene."

"But if I'm not mistaken, you didn't miss out on the Montfort weakness for the well-turned ankle and nicely rounded bosom, did you?"

Edmond narrowed his eyes.

"Drop the gun, Montfort, or the lady will be in se-erious trouble. You see, despite what you may have assumed, she tru-uly isn't involved. And you wouldn't want the death of an innocent victim on your conscience, now wou-ould you?" He pressed the cool metal of the barrel against Shelley's skin.

Edmond hesitated. Then he threw his gun to the ground.

"Now, Shelley. I want you to stay next to me as we walk out the cave—right after I dispatch some unfinished business."

"What unfinished business?" She saw him point his gun at Edmond.

"You think you know ah-all about taking care of things? Well, I'll show you something you can't take care of."

"Sorry to disagree, but you don't know the half of my capabilities." And she hauled off and backhanded him.

Lionel staggered to the side. His hands went up in the air. He dropped the flashlight.

Another body came flying through the air, and an elbow clipped Shelley in the jaw. She landed on her rump, stars flashing in front of her face.

In the darkness she heard grunting, punches, the rolling of bodies. Voices echoing in the distance.

Voices echoing in the distance?

She rubbed her jaw and shook her head. The flashlight. She had to find the flashlight.

But then she heard the shot, right next to her ear, and she went down, the back of her head cracking against the hard ground, water splattering all around her. The explosion was deafening, reverberating off the stone walls.

And then she heard nothing. Literally nothing.

She didn't think she'd been hit. She didn't feel any pain. Still, maybe she was in so much pain that her nerves had gone into shock? Shelley's brain seemed to be working in slow motion.

She lay there panting. She couldn't hear herself gasp for air, but she could feel the rise and fall of her chest. And she could tell that she was lying in the shallow underground river because she could sense the water seeping into her clothes and plastering her hair to the side of her face. It was as if she were floating in an ocean, only very cold and without any of the relaxing benefits.

She turned her head, only to experience an intense pain. And then she saw them. The lights. Bobbing through the darkness like fireflies dancing in the blackness of night.

Is this death? she wondered.

And then the lights went out.

15

SHELLEY WASN'T DEAD.

She'd merely blacked out after smacking her head on the rock. *Merely, huh.*

The noise of the gunshot fired at point-blank range—and amplified by the cave—had knocked out her hearing. It was slowly starting to come back.

Or at least this is what Paul was telling her as he shouted in her ear. He was also moving a pen flashlight back and forth between her eyes, checking for signs of a concussion.

Shelley squinted and looked around. Somehow she'd ended up sitting against a large rock just outside the entrance to the cave. "P-le-ease, would you put that thing down?" She batted his hand away. "I'm perfectly fine. And you don't need to shout."

"Well, it *is* my area of expertise," Paul replied with a harrumph and clicked off the flashlight.

"He's right, you know," Abigail said in a way that brooked no quarrel.

Shelley wasn't about to try. "What are the two of you doing here? I thought you'd be in Aix, sipping coffee and discussing the price of stemware?"

"You think our consumer needs are so great that we wouldn't be concerned?" Paul was dismayed.

"What are you talking about?"

"Right after I pulled out onto the main road—the clutch on the rental car is a little rough going from first into second, by the way—we saw these police cars barreling down in the opposite direction," Abigail explained. She was sitting on the ground next to Shelley, just daring the dust and dirt to soil her trousers. "I looked in the rearview mirror and saw them turn into the chateau. Naturally I put the car in Reverse and rushed back."

Shelley moved to get up.

Paul pressed down on her shoulder. "No, you just stay here with Abigail. I need to tend to the count. He has a flesh wound that he aggravated by insisting on moving you himself. These aristocrats—always the grand gesture. In the end, who's left to clean up the mess?" Paul stood up, squared his shoulders and strode across the path, a regular hero.

Abigail sighed. "Amazing, isn't he?" She held her chin up high. Then she looked back. "And you were something, too. Pouncing on Lionel the way you did. The count told us all about it." She patted Shelley on the head.

"Ouch." Shelley squinted.

"Well, thank goodness some of the policemen have already taken him away to jail."

That Lionel was on his way to jail was certainly a relief after what had been one of the most confusing days of her life.

But not as confusing as the way everyone—Paul, the aunts, the cops—was hanging around Edmond and hanging on to his every word.

"Shouldn't they be arresting him, too?" Shelley waggled her finger in Edmond's direction. Even that small motion made her head ache further. She dropped her arm to her side.

"Arrest the count? Shelley, what can you be thinking?"

"That everyone—including myself—has been bamboozled by an aristocratic title and a pair of startling blue eyes?"

"Shelley, Edmond is a chief inspector with the art theft division of the French National Police. He's been in charge of this case since he discovered the real Botticelli was missing last week." Abigail patted Shelley's head again. "Maybe I should have Paul examine you more thoroughly?"

Shelley batted away her hand and struggled to her feet. She wobbled and put her hand against the rock for support. Her fingers left an outline on the damp surface.

Talk about ironic.

She breathed in deeply and stared at Edmond. He was speaking to his aunts and nodding and smiling in that reassuring way he used with them. They looked relieved, and after multiple kissings of cheeks, allowed a policeman to usher them away.

Edmond glanced over. She pushed a wet lock of her hair out of her eyes. He walked toward her. "Do you mind?" he asked Abigail.

"Not at all." Abigail hurried to Paul without a backward glance.

Shelley examined Edmond. Blood covered his shirt, and there was a makeshift bandage on his arm. "You got hit?"

He glimpsed down. "It's nothing. If you hadn't punched Toynbee, it could have been worse—much worse. I owe you a great deal of thanks."

She half laughed, downplaying her bravery. "I suppose I should feel relief, too." Amazing what happened when she acted on impulse, letting her emotions rule instead of logic—first Edmond at the hotel, now Lionel in the cave.

She still wasn't sure about the consequences of either one.

"You mean you're relieved to find out that I'm not a crook?"

"Yes, well that—and that you're not a toothpaste salesman either. Not that I ever understood that. I mean, the constant phone calls—some late at night. It was all a bit bizarre."

"Yes, that was an unfortunate attempt by my aunts to try to protect me. I'd told them that the fewer people who know what I do, the better."

She nodded, causing her to shut one eye when pain knifed through her skull. "I thought it might be something like that. Anyhow, as open-minded as I'd like to think I am, I'd hate to think I'd fallen in love with a toothpaste salesman." Oops, that wasn't meant to slip out. Too late.

Edmond worked his jaw. "Here, let me help you

find your way down the path," he said by way of a non sequitur.

Well, she didn't need him to make it any clearer. Their time in Les Baux was already forgotten as far as he was concerned. In silence, she let him lead the way, and when they got to the garden wall, she stopped and cleared her throat. "Abigail tells me you've been on the case all the time."

He nodded.

She looked around, narrowing her eyes to focus on his face. "So how are Marie-Jeanne and Isabelle taking the news?"

"They were shocked to find out about the robbery but grateful that the undercover cop in the family happened to get lucky."

"Somehow I don't think luck had anything to do with it. Besides, weren't you the one who said he didn't believe in luck?"

"You listen carefully, don't you?"

Shelley looked away from his scrutiny. "Well, maybe I should have listened even better, picked up on the clues about Lionel sooner. The business with the IRS was always a little strange."

"It's not your job to be a cop."

"No, it's yours. Or should I say, an undercover chief inspector?"

"Chief inspector, cop." He shrugged. "It's all the same job."

Why did he have to be so understanding, so self-effacing? Couldn't he display some aristocratic hauteur? It would make it so much easier to hate him. So much easier to walk away without her heart being broken into tiny bits.

Shelley tossed her head back—ow, that hurt—and braved it out, trying to hate him, trying to pick up all those little pieces. "Tell me, was it part of your job to suspect me? You did, didn't you? That's what you said back in the cave?" She waited.

"In the beginning, yes. But I changed my mind yesterday at Les Baux." He stopped speaking, leaving certain things unsaid. "Then this morning, I got a call telling me that one of the workmen I'd found on a list on your computer had had dealings with Toynbee." He stopped when he saw her surprise. "Yes, while you were busy doing all the repairs around the house, I went through your things. I found the list then."

"And did you find anything else that made you suspicious?" She didn't bother to hide her displeasure.

"Not really. Just the usual stuff—clothes, underwear." He suppressed a grin. She frowned. "There were also your passport and an address book." He paused. "And the photo of your family."

"Well, that should have had you running to slap on the handcuffs." She worked the inside of her cheek.

"No, what really set me off were the phone calls I got after your friends arrived. First I learned that the FBI had uncovered that Toynbee had a gambling problem and that you periodically made out large checks to 'Cash' to pay them off."

"Those checks were to the accountant, Bernie, who was supposed to distribute them to various tax agencies." The light dawned. "Oh-h-h, I see. Some of it may have gone to Uncle Sam, but most of it went to your neighborhood loan shark."

"Exactly. And naturally I assumed that you were in on the whole thing. After all, you were the one who wrote the checks."

"Naturally." Shelley realized how easily the facts could get misconstrued. "And then the second call? What was that about?"

"That's when I received word that Toynbee had gone to the plumber's and was later spotted leaving Aix. When I saw the van, I knew he'd already arrived. The logical place to look for him was the cave, and that's when I found you—with him—and I was convinced you were in on it together."

"So when you asked me if I'd come to help him, and I said yes, you assumed I was talking about stealing the drawing, right?"

Edmond nodded.

Shelley pressed her lips together and stared down at the ground. She could plead with him, insist that she would never knowingly do anything to hurt him or his family. That one of the things she respected about him most was his sense of honor, and she hoped that in turn he recognized that in her.

But when she raised her head and studied his wary eyes, she knew that she was looking at the soul of someone whose parents' death—in front of his eyes—had left him abandoned at a young age. Even the care of his devoted aunts couldn't stem the insecurity and loss.

So in the end, she raised her chin a fraction higher and said with a smile barely turning up the corners of her mouth, "Well, if it makes you feel any better, I thought you were a crook, too—that even if you weren't the one who made the switch, you were trying to scam the insurance company or sell the original without telling your aunts. So we were both wrong."

She took a few tentative steps and wobbled.

"Are you all right?" He took her elbow.

She raised her arm away. "I'm fine. I just need a little more time to get my full bearings."

"Of course. Let me walk with you to the chateau."

And because she wasn't sure she could stand being so near to him—woman to man, man to woman, as he had put it the other day—she turned the conversation back to the crime, asking details that really didn't matter to her.

"So you found out about the fake drawing last week?" she asked.

"Yes, I discovered it when I came back to the chateau after Françoise's death. Once I ascertained that she hadn't secretly sold it, I started to track the other connections to the chateau. Dream Villas was an obvious candidate, and it turned out there had been similar incidents at other Dream Villas properties. That forgeries had been substituted for the real thing."

"And who made the forgeries?"

"A certain Mr. Bernard Waxwood."

"You're kidding? Bernie, Dream Villas' accountant? Gee, he's a regular full-service criminal kind of guy—though, it still seems, a good accountant." Shelley frowned. "Wait a minute. You mean those terrible Christmas cards he always sent?"

"Examples of his work, I'm afraid. I didn't say he was a good forger, merely a forger. After the FBI uncovered the information about the gambling debts, they got a warrant to search Dream Villas' office, and they stumbled across the cards."

"Yeah, Paul's phone message mentioned the FBI had been to Abigail's law firm. I guess that was after they'd been to Dream Villas?"

Edmond nodded. "Anyway, since this case involved art forgeries, they thought there might be a chance there was a connection. Agents were already going to bring him in on the loan-sharking charges, but when they made a visit to his residence in Cherry Hill, New Jersey, they also found various drawings and paintings, which, I'm sure upon inspection, will turn out to be tied to other Dream Villas' properties. So in the end, the fakes may have been only competent, but they were enough to buy Lionel time in making the switch for the real thing."

"It all sounds so simple."

"But you came and complicated things."

"I did, didn't I?" She managed a resigned chuckle. "And when you asked me to call Lionel and have him come over?"

Edmond was less enthusiastic to relate this part, but he owed her the truth. "I'd decided at that point that I'd been wrong and that you *were* innocent. But

I still needed to use you to lure him over in hopes of catching him with the real Botticelli drawing. He seemed anxious to have you here as a distraction, so I wanted him to know that your work was finished. Only later did I find out about the repairmen and realize he was on his way over anyway. And by that time I was convinced once more that you were in on the job."

They reached the chateau's patio. Shelley saw that Boris Spassky was still sunning himself in the giant urn. She turned to Edmond. "And what if I *had* been guilty, too? What would you have done then?" She had to know.

"Arrest you."

Again he made it all sound so simple. *No I'd have stood by you and helped you in any way I could. No, I would have been forced to do my duty because that's the kind of straight-arrow guy I am, even though it would have ripped my heart to shreds.*

No, definitely neither of those things. But then she *had* wanted the truth.

"But what I don't understand is, how did you know to look in the cave?"

"I was hoping the original might still be stashed on the grounds since with the funeral going on it would have been difficult to remove something so large with everyone milling about, and besides, there'd also been no report of anyone trying to sell it on the black market. But as to looking in the cave itself—" Edmond nodded toward the cat "—I must confess, it was due to my furry friend here. He insisted I follow him to the cave, which initially struck me as very odd, until it occurred to me that it would be an ideal place to stash the drawing. I was right. After that, it was merely a matter of switching the real one in the tube for a photocopy. Needless to say, I didn't want to risk losing it again."

Shelley glanced at Boris. He stirred from his slumber and deigned to give her an inscrutable stare. "And you said he was worthless."

"Poor judgment on my part. But I promise you I fed him royally after the discovery, which I presume was his motivation all along."

She didn't want to smile. It hurt too much. "And I also presume you *really* are broke?"

"Yes, I'm afraid so."

"So will you sell it—the chateau?" She walked over to the flower urn, bent down and smelled the heady scent of lavender and verbena.

Edmond wet his lips. "I'm not sure."

"*Monsieur l'Inspecteur*," one of the uniformed policemen called to him.

Edmond held up his hand, then turned to Shelley. His other hand was in his pocket, working the lighter. "I need to go down to the station and file a report." He motioned toward the cop. "After that, I have to check in with my bureau in Paris. I probably won't be back at the chateau tonight. Possibly not for a while. I've let other things slide because of this case, you see."

Shelley swallowed. "I see." So this was it. *La fin*, as it was written at the end of her French books. She held out her hand like a good little soldier. "Well, look after your arm, and good luck—with everything."

"You, too." The handshake was so brief, it barely qualified. "I never meant for you to be hurt, you know." A muscle in his jaw twitched.

"I'm not hurt. Just a slight bump." She touched the back of her head.

That wasn't what he'd meant.

She knew it.

He knew that she knew it.

Boris rose from the urn and stretched, arching his back. Then he hopped down and rubbed against Shelley's legs. She reached down to pet him, but the cat scampered away. "A real love-'em-and-leave-'em kind of guy." She laughed hollowly.

"So it would seem," Edmond agreed.

Shelley eyed him thoughtfully. His polo shirt was bloodied, his pants muddy and torn at a knee. There was a shiner starting to emerge below one eye and a noticeable puffiness near the side of his mouth.

It would be so easy to offer assistance, to try to make it all better. To try to fix things.

But she deserved more than that.

Instead she straightened her shoulders and stated the one fundamental truth. "It seems we have an issue with lack of trust." She didn't just mean about who was or who wasn't involved in the theft.

Edmond didn't bother to deny it. "I'd say that was right." He knew what she meant.

And then there didn't seem to be anything more for her to say.

And there didn't seem to be anything more for him to add.

Until finally, after one last glance toward the rows of almond trees on the hill, Shelley turned and said, "One more thing."

"Yes?" He waited.

And she did for a moment, too. But nothing came.

So she shrugged her shoulders. "Someone should go to the gallery and tell Marius he can stop guarding the fake Botticelli."

16

SHELLEY WAS ON ALL FOURS, holding one of her fuzzy bunny slippers and looking under the dust ruffle of her bed for the other.

It might be eighty degrees out, but she was frozen. Even wearing sweatpants, a sweatshirt, wool socks and one slipper didn't seem to ward off the chill.

Dammit. She needed that other slipper.

She hadn't been able to get warm since returning to the States. Maybe loss of body heat was directly related to unemployment?

With Lionel in the clink and Dream Villas' accounts put on hold, she was scrambling around looking for work. Desperate but not too proud, she had put in an application for a job at her local Starbucks. They couldn't pay any worse than Lionel, she figured, and there was the side benefit of free coffee.

She was still waiting to hear from them. She had long ago given up waiting to hear from anyone else.

As it turned out, she *had* gotten a flight out the next day. But alone. Abigail and Paul had decided to stay on for a long weekend in Nice. "Mummy always said the Riviera in spring was *the* time to come," Abigail had said from the driver's seat of Shelley's rental car. Sitting in the passenger seat, Paul had been studying the map until Abigail took it from him.

Shelley knew they were probably having a very nice time. Abigail would drive and give directions while Paul could comment on all the strange foreign noses.

Far more troubling was the phone call she had gotten from Marie-Jeanne and Isabelle the day after she had returned. They'd been concerned that Edmond had done something to drive her away. They had called him in Paris several times. Never mind the critical nature of his work, "He simply shouldn't treat so lovely a young lady as yourself in such an untoward manner," they had said Isabelle was of half a mind never to make his favorite madeleines anymore unless he corrected this frightful breach of etiquette.

Shelley had assured them that Edmond had had nothing to do with her sudden departure. Rather it had been the necessity of getting her life in order, in view of her changed circumstances.

It was true. She wasn't so much running away as determined to face reality as quickly as possible. Unlike her mother, buried in her bromeliads, Shelley was going to go boldly into the night—and day.

She now understood that she was meant to be among people, that she enjoyed it and that she was good at it. But she also knew that the first person she needed to take care of was herself. Ergo, she was going to go out and do something that made her happy. Whether happiness also included a steady relationship was something she'd tackle later.

And she would—eventually. Because one positive thing that had come out of the whole fiasco with Edmond de Montfort was the realization—the acceptance, really—that she was attractive. Desirable, even.

And that she shouldn't just settle for second best. She deserved more.

Her hand came to rest on something. "*Voilà!*" She pulled it out. "Oh, damn." It was a long scarf, which her mother had knitted for Christmas.

"Do not be discouraged with little setbacks," she lectured herself. "If life hands you lemons, make lemonade." With those words in mind, she wrapped the scarf around her neck and prayed that she would soon stop sounding like *Poor Richard's Almanac*.

The buzzer sounded outside her door.

Shelley trudged to the living room and looked through the peephole. "I don't believe it." She made a frantic attempt to tuck her hair behind her ears. "Oh, why do I bother?" she muttered and swung open the door.

"The list of repairmen is in the kitchen in a vase, tucked in with the wooden spoons," she announced.

"That's not why I came, though the pool filter does seem to have stopped working."

Shelley almost closed the door on him there and then, except that his foot, shod in a marvelous Italian loafer—which she was surprised to see was polished and not in the slightest need of repair—was stuck in the doorjamb.

"May I?" He nodded to come in.

She stepped to the side and made a large sweeping motion with her hand. Until she saw it was the one holding the bunny slipper, which she hastily deposited next to the coatrack.

Edmond walked inside and placed a plastic bag with the words Duty-Free printed on it on a chair. He surveyed her tiny apartment. "Cozy," he pronounced.

"If you mean its total square footage is smaller than the laundry room at the chateau, I'd say you were fairly accurate."

He walked around and patted the back of the sofa. She'd found it abandoned on the street and wrestled it home and up the stairs. The blue Indian-print bedspread covering it could never be confused with Waverly fabric at sixty-five dollars a yard.

He stopped by the table and pointed at the drooping plant in the middle.

"A present from my mother." She eyed him critically as he peered at a small engraving hung on the wall. "It's Dutch, nineteenth century, bought at auction with my first paycheck from Dream Villas. I lived on Corn Flakes for a month as a result. I have the documentation, if you'd like to see it."

"No, that won't be necessary." He stood up straight and turned to face her. "As I said, very cozy."

"It's nice to know you approve." She waited for him to offer some explanation for the visit.

None came.

And she got tired of the waiting game. "So, other

than choosing to grace me with your keen eye for decoration, what brings you to the City of Brotherly Love?"

Edmond reached for the shopping bag. "I have it on good authority that a particularly fine medieval ivory is no longer hanging in the gallery at the Montfort chateau."

"Well, you've come to the wrong place," she said, teed off. "Besides, I have it on good authority that France has strict regulations about taking artwork out of the country."

"Which is why it's probably a good thing that a police inspector was the one transporting it." He took a package out of the bag and gently removed the bubble wrap.

Shelley stepped forward when she saw what it was. "The ivory? You took it?"

"Let's just say I have connections." He held it out. "It's for you."

Shelley placed her hand on her chest. "For me? I don't understand."

"The aunts said it was the least I could do after treating you so abominably. They even threatened to throw both me and Boris Spassky out of the house. I couldn't do that to the cat, now could I?"

She held the small tablet in her hands and gazed at it lovingly. "It's very generous—"

For one brief, shining moment it was hers.

"—but I can't accept it." She gave it back to him. "Please tell Marie-Jeanne and Isabelle that it was so like them to remember how much I admired the piece, but no, thank you. They'll just **have** to take

Boris Spassky back, no matter what. As for you, they can make up their own minds." She shook her head. "I still can't believe you flew all the way here just to placate your aunts."

"Did I mention that the pool filter is broken?"

"I believe you said something about it."

There was an awkward silence.

"I've decided not to sell the chateau—or at least to do everything that I can to avoid having to do that. I've already had several appraisers in to look at the art, as well as some of the manuscripts."

"And the Botticelli?"

"We are fortunate that the original is of much better quality than the forgery. It will bring a considerable amount." He smiled resolutely. "In addition, *Tante* Isabelle and *Tante* Marie-Jeanne have contacted that vintage-clothing dealer you suggested in Beverly Hills, and apparently their Elsa Schiaparelli gowns alone will contribute nicely toward working down the debt."

"And they don't mind selling off their clothes?"

"Not at all, especially since you introduced them to online shopping at Lands' End. Now all they talk about is polar-fleece this and polar-fleece that."

Shelley bit back a smile.

Edmond held up a hand, hesitated a moment and clenched it. "They miss you. Marius misses you—so much that I have to remind him to water the flowers. The Miele repairman, Toto, even mopes around the place, finding excuses to check the coils in the refrigerator." He paused and plunged his hand in his pants pocket. Drat, just when he needed his lighter most, it wasn't there, a victim of airline security.

All right, he'd just have to say it without the aid of props. "*I* miss you."

Shelley rubbed her shoulder and quickly realized that she was wearing the ten-foot-long powder-blue scarf. She dropped her arms to her side. "That's not good enough."

Edmond took a step forward, then thought better of it. He ran his hand through his hair. He'd gotten it cut for the occasion, and as a result, his gesture made it stand up like wounded tufts of puppy fur.

"They love you," he said and swallowed. "And I love you." He swallowed again. "And I trust you—without qualification."

Shelley was stunned. Only a few days ago, if he'd said the exact same thing, she'd have thrown herself at him, secure in the belief that they would live happily ever after. Today, she no longer had the wool over her eyes.

Instead, it was wound around her neck.

Today, she was waiting to hear about a job application at Starbucks.

"For Pete's sake," she answered. "You're a count."

Edmond shifted on his feet. This is not what he'd expected to hear. "But I'm also a cop."

"Edmond, do you understand my status in life? I'm officially out of work."

"So? I may have a title, but I'm broke."

Shelley groaned. "Edmond, you're a fantasy, you're not real."

"I'm here in Philadelphia, in this apartment, aren't I?" He waved his hand around. He seemed to be doing a lot of that lately.

"It doesn't matter, Edmond. You and I don't belong to the same worlds."

"'If you prick me, do I not bleed?'"

Shelley grabbed her head. "P-le-ase, don't start quoting Shakespeare to me. My mother was an English teacher—I recognize *The Merchant of Venice* when I hear it."

"Do you know this one? 'If loaded items are not acceptably dried, check to see that the exhaust duct is clean and not blocked.'"

Shelley's mouth dropped open. "That's part of the instructions for using the dryer."

He smiled hopefully. "I know. I'm learning all about things like dryers in your absence."

Exasperated, Shelley dropped her arms to her sides. "How can I say this simply? You, Edmond, Count de Montfort—and everything that your name and title connote—are a fantasy. You can't base a long-lasting relationship on a fantasy."

"If it makes you feel any better, you could call me Ed?"

"Argh!" She stormed over to her window and looked at the street below. She sensed him come stand behind her, but she refused to turn around. She crossed her arms and hugged her chest.

"Shelley, coming to see you was so important that I made sure nothing would interfere with it. I refused to bring my mobile phone."

She shrugged. "That's a start."

"Not only that, I didn't even inform my office where I'd be." He inhaled slowly. "Doesn't that tell you something about the depth of my feelings that I'm out of touch with the world of dental floss, not to mention high crimes and misdemeanors?"

That had Shelley thinking. She looked down at the scarf. It was supposed to have the letters *U P* for University of Pennsylvania stitched into the wool, but her mother's feeble knitting ability rendered it more like a smiley face without the smile. Maybe if she took a bit of extra yarn, she could fix it—

Shelley picked up the end of the scarf and stared more closely at the misshapen letters. "I don't believe it. To think, my mother has provided insight into human behavior."

Without any preamble or explanation, she swung around and started inspecting Edmond, holding up one sleeve of his linen jacket, pushing it back to check his cuff, then dropping it and repeating the same process with his other arm. They seemed to meet her satisfaction. Next she held open the sides of his jacket and moved her head up and down.

"If you're looking for a small box containing the Montfort emerald-and-diamond ring, traditionally referred to as the Band of Tears and Joy—this *is* a Montfort heirloom after all, with all that it connotes—it's in the inside pocket of my jacket."

Shelley stilled her hands. "You don't say?"

"I do say." The corners of his mouth—that very sexy mouth—tweaked up.

She smiled. "That's very nice to know. And it's especially nice to know that the stones aren't arranged in the shape of a porcupine, but that's not what I'm after at the moment."

Edmond was confused. "You're not?"

"Bend your head down," she ordered.

"Bend my head down?" But he dutifully leaned over.

"More. I'm not standing on stilts, you know."

He stooped over and patiently tolerated her checking the back of his neck. "I promise I washed behind my ears." There was amusement in his voice but also a little uncertainty.

"That's all right. You can straighten up now." Shelley backed off and crossed her arms. "I am delighted to see that there isn't a single button missing or a frayed collar in sight."

"For you, I cleaned up." Edmond loosened the back of his shirt collar, which, even though the top two buttons were undone, felt strangely tight. He furrowed his brow. "Shelley, I didn't want you to think you had to take care of me or feel obliged constantly to fix things."

Shelley breathed in deeply and felt contentment envelope her. She hadn't felt this happy and this at ease since…since forever. "Edmond." She hesitated. "My sweetheart. Not only am I delighted that you didn't split an infinitive, I can't thank you enough for your kindness and understanding. I also think your decision to hold on to the chateau is very noble—and not entirely foolhardy. I am convinced you can still rent out the chateau at exorbitant prices—I, after all, have the contacts and the know-how."

"Absolutely, I couldn't agree more." Edmond seemed to rise a little taller in his shined shoes. "And you'd be willing to do that—for a salary, of course?"

"Only on a short-term basis." She could see the light dim in his eyes. "Because in the long term, in addition to the idea of opening the caves to sensitively minded tourism, I think we should convert the chateau into an exclusive mini retirement home. I find I quite like old people—they appreciate the beauty and importance of things past. And they should be able to live comfortably in that kind of environment instead of in some sterile, cookie-cutter old-age home.

"The Mother Theresa of retirees." When he saw her reaction, he held up his hands in surrender. "I mean that as a compliment. I do, truly I do."

Shelley smiled, liking the ring to that last sentence. Still, she wasn't about to let him off the hook quite yet. "So?"

"So?" He looked confused. "Oh, yes. I think it's a great idea. I've been worried that my aunts were getting too isolated, and I think it would be wonderful to have others with whom they could interact. I can see Isabelle giving cooking classes and Marie-Jeanne organizing a mystery-book group. It would be perfect—idyllic even—especially with you there."

"That's nice to hear, but it's not what I meant when I said 'so.'"

"It's not?" He could speak four modern languages

and two ancient ones fluently, but for the life of him, Edmond didn't know what Shelley was talking about.

"About this trust thing?" she ventured. He nodded. "Do you really mean it—I mean, really and truly? I know how difficult it is for you."

Edmond closed his eyes and breathed in slowly. He pictured Shelley looking for her shoe. He remembered her gazing in wonder at the cave paintings. And he recalled in total detail the way she looked naked. "Yes," he said with certitude and opened his eyes on the woman he loved. "I trust you with my family's heritage." He indicated the ivory. "And I trust you with my heart—really and truly."

He waited. "Shelley?"

Oh, he said her name so beautifully. She cleared her throat and stood up straight. *Mademoiselle* Bruce would have been proud. "Now that that's settled, would you mind coming over *here?*" She pointed in front of her.

"Here, as in here?" Edmond tentatively stepped forward.

"Nowhere else," she said, putting her arms around his shoulders and linking her hands behind his neck. She felt the tension begin to seep from his muscles.

"Does this mean what I think it means?"

"That I love you, that I want you, that I trust you implicitly. That I'll think about looking into the pool filter provided you take charge of all appliance repairs. I'm not sure I can face Toto again."

He smiled that great smile of his that had his dimples creasing and his eyes twinkling, not to mention Shelley's insides going all mush, just as they'd done that first day at Chateau d'If when she'd seen him appear, haloed by the sun.

No, not like that day. Because today Edmond de Montfort wasn't a fantasy but flesh and blood. Yes, he was sometimes irritating, but he and he alone could mark her soul forever. Her imperfect hero.

"Ed," she said, mentally congratulating herself that she had vacuumed the living room rug just that morning. "I'm all yours."

La fin

HARLEQUIN
flipside

Be sure to catch your favorite
Harlequin Flipside authors
writing for other Silhouette
and Harlequin series!

SILHOUETTE *Romance*®

Holly Jacobs
in Silhouette Romance

ONCE UPON A PRINCESS
May 2005

ONCE UPON A PRINCE
July 2005

ONCE UPON A KING
September 2005

Also watch for:
Stephanie Doyle in Silhouette Bombshell in July 2005
Elizabeth Bevarly, Cindi Myers and Dawn Atkins
appearing in Harlequin Blaze in Fall 2005
Stephanie Rowe writing for Harlequin Intrigue in 2006
Barbara Dunlop in Silhouette Desire in 2006

Look for books by these authors at your favorite retail outlet.

www.eHarlequin.com   HFAIOS

Are you getting it
at least twice a month?

Here's how: Try RED DRESS INK books
on for size & receive two FREE gifts!

Bombshell
by Lynda Curnyn

As Seen on TV
by Sarah Mlynowski

YES! Send my two FREE books.
There's no risk and no purchase required—ever!

Name (PLEASE PRINT)

Address   Apt. #

City   State/Prov.   Zip/Postal Code

Want to try another series? Call 1-800-873-8635
or order online at www.TryRDI.com/free.

RED
DRESS
INK™

RDI04MMP